"The Kid Who Would Be King"

One-Minute Bible Stories About Kids

"The Kid Who Would Be King"

One-Minute Bible Stories About Kids

Written by Marnie Wooding
Illustrated by Chris Kielesinski

HOLMAN
BIBLE PUBLISHERS

Nashville, Tennessee

Library of Congress Cataloging-in-Publication Data
Wooding, Marnie
    The kid who would be king : one minute Bible stories about kids / written by Marnie Wooding ; illustrated by Chris Kielesinski.
        p. cm.
    ISBN 0-8054-9399-9 (alk. paper)
    1. Bible stories, English [1. Bible stories] I. Kielesinski, Chris, ill. II. Title.

BS551.2 .W62 2000
220.9'505—dc21
                                                      00-036111

Bibliography of Sources
After School Weird Stuff Brain Quest. New York: Workman Publishing Company, 1996.
"Encarta 98," CD-ROM Microsoft Corporation.
Matthews, Peter and Norris McWhirter. *The Guinness Book of Records 1993*. Middlesex, England: Guinness Publishing, 1993.
Matthews, Victor H. *Manners and Customs in the Bible*. Rev. ed. Peabody, Massachusetts: Hendrickson Publishers Inc, 1996.
Millard, Alan. *Nelson's Illustrated Wonders and Discoveries of the Bible*. Nashville: Thomas Nelson Publishers, 1997.
Penwell, Dan. *Bible Brain Quest 1,000 Questions & Answers About the Old & New Testaments*. New York: Workman Publishing Company, 1997.
Rosenbloom, Joseph. *The Little Giant Book of Riddles*. New York: Sterling Publishing Co. Inc., 1996.
Seyffert, Oskar. *Dictionary of Classical Antiquities*. Cleveland: Meridian Books, 1969.
Wallechinsky, David and Amy Wallace. *The Book of Lists*. Boston: Little, Brown and Company, 1995.
Werner, Keller. *The Bible As History*. 2nd Rev. ed. New York: Bantam Books, 1988.
The Youth Bible—New Century Version. Dallas: Word Publishing, 1991.

Printed in Korea
1 2 3 4 5 04 03 02 01 00
SW

Contents

Introduction

Hi there! Great to see you! I'm your narrator, and I've been waiting for you to open this book! The Introduction is the beginning of the book, so I thought it would be the perfect time to get to know one another. What's a narrator? Well, I'm the person who explains the stories (Bible stories in this case) in a funny and approachable way. (The publisher told me to say that.) What I'm really here for, is for us to have a great time learning about kids in the Bible.

There were some really cool guys and girls who lived back in the olden days—Bible times. They had adventures and fought giants (like this kid named David), solved royal mysteries (like this other guy named Joseph), and even freed an entire nation from slavery (like Moses). You see, this Moses was floating down the river called the Nile, and then his sister Miriam . . . Huh? Oh, sorry. I'm getting ahead of myself.

During our journey back in time, we can learn some important verses from the Bible, figure out some mysteries like what that's got to do with you, and ask a few puzzling questions. I'm also going to tell you a few jokes along the way. (Just a note for the future—if you, the reader, laugh at the narrator's jokes, it always makes the narrator feel good about herself. Cheering and clapping are, of course, optional.)

Enough talking already, why don't we just check it out? Let's start at the beginning of the Bible with the book called Genesis. That makes sense. Right? There was this boy named Isaac . . .

The Trust Test

"Your hearts must be fully with the Lord our God, to walk in His laws and to keep His commandments, as on this day" (1 Kings 8:61).

People lived a pretty simple life back in the times of the book of Genesis. They didn't have computer games, television, or microwaves. I know, it's hard to believe, but true. They were shepherds and moved from place to place finding fresh pastureland for their sheep and goats. Anyway, this couple named Abraham and Sarah had prayed for a long time to have a child of their own, but years passed and still no baby. By now they were really old—I mean, Abraham was already a hundred. But, they didn't let a little thing like old age stop them from praying to God. God heard their prayers and gave them a son. Boy, were they ever happy! Abraham called him Isaac.

Before you knew it, Isaac had grown to be a pretty great kid and was old enough to help herd the animals. Isaac probably memorized everything his father taught him and knew exactly where the sweet grass grew and where the best watering holes could be found. Life was good!

One day God called to Abraham, not with a phone or anything, He just said, "'Abraham!'

"'Here I am,' he replied.

JOKE

What did Abraham call the ram that he saw in the thicket?

"Hiram!"

"Then God said, 'Take your son, your only son, Isaac, whom you love, and go to the land of Moriah, and offer him there as a burnt offering on one of the mountains that I will show you'" (Genesis 22:1–2).

Hold the phone a second. It was hard to believe, but God had just asked Abraham to take his boy Isaac up to a mountain and kill him as an offering to God. Fairly drastic stuff. Could this really be true? Read on.

As you can imagine, Isaac must have been very excited when his dad told him they were going on a trip together. But Abraham didn't tell Isaac what God had said. They saddled up a donkey, took two servants and a whole lot of firewood, and set out for the mountain. On the third day, Abraham saw the exact mountain God had told him about. *Abraham said to his servants,*

'Stay here with the donkey. The boy and I will go over there and worship, and then we will return to you'" (Genesis 22:5).

Isaac helped his father carry the firewood, but perhaps his father's sadness made him wonder about their trip. At any rate, it seems he got thinking.

"Isaac said to Abraham his father, 'Father!'

"'Yes, my son,' he answered.

"'The fire and wood are here,' said Isaac, 'but where is the lamb for the burnt offering?'

"Abraham replied, 'My son, God Himself will provide the lamb for a burnt offering.' So the two of them walked on together" (Genesis 22:7–8). This is just so sad!

"When they came to the place God had told him about, Abraham built an altar there and arranged the wood. Then he bound his son Isaac and put him on top of the wood on the altar" (Genesis 22:9).

Put yourself in Isaac's place. Would you have been frightened if your father tied your hands and feet, and laid you on an altar? Well, maybe Isaac was frightened, but he did exactly what his father asked! I guess he trusted his father, probably because he knew how much Abraham loved him.

Even though I'm sure Abraham's heart was breaking, *"Abraham reached out and took the knife to slaughter his son. But the Angel of the Lord called to him from heaven: 'Abraham! Abraham!'*

"'Here I am,' he answered.

"Then He said, 'Don't lay a hand on the boy or do anything to him. For now I

know that you fear God, since you haven't withheld your only son from Me'" (Genesis 22:10–12).

How long do you think it took Abraham to untie Isaac? The Bible doesn't tell us, but I have a feeling some speed records were broken that day. *"Then Abraham looked up and saw in the distance a ram caught in a thicket by its horns"* (Genesis 22:13)—you know . . . a boy sheep.

Isaac watched as his relieved father went over and took the ram and sacrificed it as a burnt offering. Abraham called the mountain, *"The Lord Provides"* (Genesis 22:14).

But wait! The story's not over yet. *"The Angel of the Lord called to Abraham from heaven a second time: 'I Myself have pledged,' declares the Lord, 'because you have done this, and have not withheld your* only son, I will certainly bless you, and I will greatly multiply your descendants as the stars of heaven and the sand that is on the seashore; and your descendants will take possession of the gate of their enemies; and all the nations of the earth will be blessed through your descendants because you have obeyed My voice'" (Genesis 22:15–18). Wow, that's one big promise!

Why would God put Abraham and Isaac through such a tough trust test? It seems God wanted to know if Abraham would trust Him and if he would be obedient. Abraham absolutely passed the test. And Isaac passed his test too.

God loves us and we have to trust Him with our lives and take care of the

DIDYAKNOW?

Isaac may have thought grasshoppers were a tasty snack.

people we love. I doubt God really wanted Abraham to harm Isaac. After all, God loved Isaac too. But Abraham's actions showed his strong faith in God. How can you show your love for God? What kind of sacrifices can you make? Tough questions.

There will come a time in your life when God may ask you to sacrifice your own desires and needs for Him. For example, say you were invited to go to your friend's ski cabin for a long weekend of snowboarding. But this was the coldest December on record and your church was opening its doors to the homeless. Your parents volunteered to spend the weekend passing out blankets, making hot soup, and pouring gallons of coffee. They didn't ask you to give up your weekend, but there was that little voice inside you asking, "Hey, do you think that could be God talking to you?" Before you know it, you could be passing out cookies and making sandwiches!

You may never know what a difference you could make in someone's life by just being there with a warm blanket, but God does, and He would be so very proud of you! Way to go!

QUESTION CORNER

* Would God ever ask you to do something wrong? How do you know?
* Why do you think God tests us?
* Has God ever "tested" you? What happened?

Joseph's Journey

"You meant evil against me; God meant it for good, to save many people's lives as it is happening today" (Genesis 50:20).

If there was a teenager in all of Canaan who seemed to have everything going for him, it was Joseph. He was smart and good-looking, and was loved by everybody who knew him—well, almost everybody. You see, he was his father's favorite son and got special treatment. His ten brothers wanted to treat him special too, but I don't think in a nice way. His father Jacob gave him a beautiful coat, which made his brothers jealous.

To make matters worse, Joseph had amazing dreams. He dreamed that he and his brothers were sheaves of grain, but Joseph's was tall and proud while his brothers' were smaller and bowed down to his. This dream didn't go over well with the bros.

Not long after that, Joseph had another dream very much like the first. Now that was the last straw! His brothers decided to make "Mr. Fancy Coat" an ex-brother.

One day his father sent him out to check on them as they tended the flock. *"They said to one another, 'Here comes that master dreamer! Come on, let's kill him, and throw him into one of the cisterns [water wells]. We can say, "A wild animal has devoured him." Then we'll see what becomes of his dreams'"* (Genesis 37:19–20).

However, after discussing it, the brothers decided instead to sell Joe as a slave to a caravan of Ishmaelite merchants bound for Egypt. The brothers tore Joseph's coat, dipped it in goat's blood, and told their father some animal had killed him. Naturally Jacob was heartbroken.

Joseph was taken to Egypt and sold to a man named Potiphar who was the king's captain of the guards. As slaves go, Joseph was a rookie, but Potiphar was an okay guy, and Joseph worked hard for his master. He probably counted the silver, fed the dogs, and groomed the camels. He did it all. I guess he figured if you have to be a slave, why not be the BEST. God blessed Joseph in everything he did so that soon he had worked his way up to being Potiphar's personal

DIDYAKNOW?
Joseph was only seventeen when his adventures started.

assistant. You certainly can't beat a good middle management job! Unfortunately, Joseph had problems with Potiphar's flirty wife. He tried to avoid her, but her lies finally landed him in jail.

Joe may have felt like a depressed failure, but once again God blessed him and soon he was the warden's favorite— a model prisoner. *"The prison warden put Joseph in charge of all the inmates in the prison"* (Genesis 39:22)! You just can't keep a good man down.

While Joseph was in jail, he met two royal servants who had displeased the king. Both men had strange dreams in jail, but God showed Joseph the dreams' meanings. The cupbearer would

JOKE

Who was the first tennis player in history? *Joseph, because he served in Pharaoh's court.*

return to his royal duties, but the baker was . . . well, toast. Pretty crumby, but Joe was right!

Two years later Pharaoh, the ruler of Egypt, had some pretty odd dreams himself. Kingly dream number one— seven fat, healthy cows grazed by the Nile. Then seven skinny, ugly cows appeared and ate the seven good cows. Talk about your Big Mac attack! His second dream was similar. These dreams were giving Pharaoh a royal headache until the cupbearer remembered Joseph's amazing ability to interpret dreams. Before you could say, "Morning Joe," our boy, all squeaky clean, was standing before Pharaoh. Joseph explained Pharaoh's dreams. God was warning that there would be seven good years of harvest followed by seven years of no harvests. Joseph even suggested a smart savings plan. Pharaoh was very impressed, and before you know it, Joseph was second-in-command in all the land. Pharaoh gave Joseph a new life with all the royal trimmings: from prison to palace—not bad for one morning's work.

Joseph was a good manager and soon had one-fifth of the produce from the good seven years' harvest stored safely for the years of famine ahead.

The famine hit Joseph's family pretty hard back in Canaan. To keep the family from starving, ten brothers went to Egypt to buy grain. They were brought before Joseph, but they didn't even recognize their successful, superstar brother. If they had, they would have been scared to death! But even after all they had done to him, Joseph still loved his brothers. And though he had no desire to take revenge on them, Joseph wanted to test them, so he didn't reveal who he really was. He accused them of being spies. The brothers insisted they were honest men and bowed low to him just as his boyhood dreams had foretold. Joseph agreed to sell them grain, but he had a few requests of his own. He ordered them to bring back to Egypt his youngest brother Benjamin. The worried Canaan crew agreed.

On their second visit to Egypt, Joseph hid a silver cup in Benjamin's sack to test his brothers' honesty. Then he ordered his servant to stop and search them. Sure enough, they found the royal cup. Joseph acted absolutely outraged and ordered that innocent Benjamin be made a slave. His older brother Judah offered to take Ben's place. Joseph was touched by

DIDYAKNOW?
The average person has around one to two hours worth of dreams a night.

19

the good changes in his brothers and decided to tell them who he really was.

"Joseph said to his brothers, . . . 'I am Joseph your brother, whom you sold into Egypt. But don't be grieved or angry with yourselves that you sold me here, because God sent me ahead of you to preserve life. . . . It was not you who sent me here, but God. He has made me father to Pharaoh, a master of all his house, and a ruler in all the land of Egypt!" (Genesis 45:4–5, 8). Wow, now that's a godly long-term plan! Joseph invited the entire Canaan clan to come join him in his prosperity. Even Pharaoh loved the idea of a big family reunion.

It's easy to see that God had a plan for Joseph from the very beginning. Although it may not have been easy for Joe to keep his faith strong during the tough times, he always followed God and did his best in every circumstance.

That's an example we can all follow.

Often it's hard to see God's plan in our own lives. But no matter where you are, what you're doing, or how you feel about what you're doing—trust in God. Even if life seems to have hit some rocky roads, God has everything in control. Our job is to keep living the way God wants us to and then leave the rest to Him. If God can take Joseph out of a prison and into a palace, just imagine what He can do for you!

QUESTION CORNER

- What do you think God's plan for you is?
- How do you know when you are following God's plan?
- What difficult circumstances do you face? How can you serve God with them?

Moses & Miriam Making Their Mark

"The Lord will protect him and keep him alive; he will be blessed on the earth, and You will not deliver him to the wishes of his enemies" (Psalm 41:2).

Many years (or should I say pages) had passed since Joseph was in charge of Egypt, and many generations of Israelites had grown up and passed away. During their time in Egypt, the Israelites had grown into a large nation and had prospered (after all they had a good teacher in Joe). In fact they were *too* successful and numerous for one new Egyptian king. He feared their growing power and strength. *"They put bosses over them to*

21

mistreat them in their forced work. . . . But the more they mistreated them, the more they multiplied and grew. And the Egyptians came to hate and fear the Israelites. So the Egyptians made the Israelites work very hard. They made their lives bitter with hard work, in mortar, in brick, and in all kinds of field work" (Exodus 1:11–14). When hard work didn't decrease the number of Israelites, Pharaoh decided to kill every newborn Israelite boy.

DIDYAKNOW?

The Israelites didn't build the pyramids. They built treasure cities. The pyramids were already 1,500 years old at the time.

But one Hebrew mother and father decided not to obey. Instead, they kept their baby boy hidden for three months. Of course, you can't hide a baby forever, so the mother had to come up with a more permanent plan. *"She got a basket for him made of papyrus leaves and waterproofed with pitch. She put the child in it, and placed it in among the reeds by the bank of the Nile River"* (Exodus 2:3). The desperate mother watched as her son drifted down the river and out of her life. Can you imagine her fear as the tiny reed basket floated alone in the huge Nile River ready to be run over by sailboats (called *feluccas*) or snatched by hungry crocodiles? What would happen to the little baby inside?

Well, the baby had a clever sister named Miriam. She ran along the banks of the muddy river and followed the basket to see what would happen to her baby brother. She must have pushed through the heavy papyrus reeds and sent river ducks flapping across the water as she tried to keep the basket in

sight. What if it floated across the Nile to the other side? What would she do? But the river current pushed the basket closer to shore among the tall reeds. The baby came to rest in the most perfect spot in the entire river. What Miriam saw probably amazed and frightened her.

"The daughter of Pharaoh came down to wash herself at the river, and her servant girls walked along by the river's bank. When she saw the basket among the reeds, she sent her servant to get it. And when she opened it, she saw the baby" (Exodus 2:5–6). Talk about a royal encounter of the godly kind! Little Miriam probably watched with wide eyes as the royal princess herself held the little slave baby. *"There he was, crying. She felt sorry for him and said, 'This is one of the Hebrew babies!'"* (Exodus 2:6). Miriam must have held her breath; would the princess have her brother killed?

Now big sister was very brave and smart. Miriam had a great plan and, I think, she prayed that it would work. Even though she was just a poor slave girl, she bravely approached the royal party. She must have known she could be killed for such a bold act, but she spoke right up to Pharaoh's daughter!

"Should I go and get you a Hebrew woman to nurse the baby for you?"

"Pharaoh's daughter said to her, 'Go'" (Exodus 2:7–8). With pounding heart, Miriam must have raced back to her mother. I think her mother could hardly believe it as they ran along the riverbank to meet the princess. Would this mean her son was truly safe?

JOKE

How do babies swim? *They do the crawl.*

24

"Pharaoh's daughter said to her, 'Take this baby and nurse him for me, and I will pay you.' So the woman took the baby, and nursed him" (Exodus 2:9).

Amazing! God saved the baby from death and placed him under the protection of the princess. And now his mother could keep her baby with her— if only for a short time. To top it all off, Pharaoh's household, the man who ordered the baby's death, was going to pay for the baby's family to raise him! God has a great sense of humor and justice! Talk about a royal Pharaoh failure.

The boy stayed safely with his mother, probably until he was three to five years old. *"And the child grew and she brought him to Pharaoh's daughter, and he became her son. She named him Moses, and explained, 'It is because I pulled him out of the water'"* (Exodus 2:10).

Moses sure had a bright future ahead of him, and his sister Miriam had a big role to play in making that future happen. With God's help she was wise and bold beyond her years. By seizing the moment and putting aside her own safety and fears, she had become a genuine hero!

Hey, let's take a closer look at Moses' mighty smart older sister. I figure Miriam did what she did because she loved her brother. Even though she was young, she took an active role in helping her family. Family is an important part of our lives. God has carefully placed us in the care of people who love us. Being in a family isn't a one-way street of people doing things

DIDYAKNOW?
The Nile, at 4,145 miles long, is one of the two longest rivers in the world.

for us. Miriam certainly showed her love and care for her family.

How can we make the people in our lives feel special? We can start by simply treating everybody at home the way we would want to be treated—with respect, kindness, and love! Remember, friends may come and go, but brothers and sisters are for life!

We should honor our parents by responsibly doing our duties at school and home. We should obey the rules of the house, because they are there to keep us safe. It doesn't matter who is taking care of us, whether it is our parents, older siblings, grandparents, or others. Remember, they have more experience in life and with God. And most importantly, they love us! Our families and God are part of our success team and our helpers in having good lives. God gave us families to love because He loved us first and taught us how to love! So look for ways to show your family your love.

QUESTION CORNER

* If you have a brother or sister or cousin, how can you be a Miriam to them?
* How can you make your family relationships closer?
* How has God looked after you?

Samson's Head Start

Who hasn't heard of the amazing strong man named Samson? He was big, he was powerful, he was muscular. But did he start out that way? Of course not. Just like everybody else, he started out small—baby-size small, that is.

Times were tough for Samson's parents before he was born. You see, many tribes of people traveled and settled in the land of Canaan. Everybody wanted a spot for themselves in this land of plenty, and that led to plenty of trouble. Each tribe wanted to be boss. One group, the Philistines, often battled with the Israelites over cities, land, water rights, and so on. Imagine planting and growing your crops only to have some Philistine thugs take all your harvest, leaving you and your family to starve. It was a constant tug-of-war between the two communities, but the Philistines were a powerful group with more advanced metal weapons. For forty years before Samson's birth, the Philistines had ruled over the Israelites. Because of the differences in religious beliefs and just everyday living, it wasn't easy for people like Samson's mother and father to live side by side with their enemies.

DIDYAKNOW?
Both Samson and King David killed a lion.

But in times of difficulty, God often provided Israel with amazing heroes. One day an angel appeared to a Hebrew woman. The Bible doesn't tell us she was frightened, so maybe this angel looked like an ordinary guy. But there was something special about him because she did know he was a tourist of the heavenly kind. The angel told her, *"Look, you've never been able to have a child, but you will . . . have a son"* (Judges 13:3). This wasn't going to be any ordinary boy; in fact, he was a hero in the making. The angel gave her some very important instructions. She wasn't to drink wine or any other alcoholic beverage; she was only to eat foods that were prepared in agreement with the Laws of Moses; and, after the baby was born, she was never to cut or shave his hair. From day one this was going to be a special

child and, not to get all hairy about it, one with really, really long hair. And he'd be strong. I mean he'd have to be, just to carry all that hair around!

Why all these rules? Well, I think it was one way for God to see how obedient and serious Samson's parents were in following His will in all things. Besides, God wanted this baby to be trained in doing only right things from the day he was born until the day he died. You see, God had a plan to make Samson an important person in helping His people get free of the Philistines' rule and in teaching those big bullying Philistines a lesson in the social graces. It just isn't

DIDYAKNOW?

Human hair grows at the average rate of half an inch per month. Some of the longest documented hair is over 12 feet long!

very polite going around raiding your neighbors all the time.

"The woman had a son and named him Samson. The child grew and the Lord blessed him" (Judges 13:24). Everything was going just fine! Our little family was raising Samson exactly the way God wanted.

The Bible even tells us that *"the Spirit of the Lord began to work in him"* (Judges 13:25). What does that mean exactly? God was working in Samson's life in a big way already, and had given him certain gifts or abilities. God had a job or mission all planned out for Samson, and God never gives a mission without providing the right tools to do the job. What were Samson's tools? He was amazingly strong, brave, and here's the key: he had God in his corner.

Of course, there is no point in

being big, bulky, and strong if you don't know how to use your strength correctly. So as Samson grew from a baby to a man, I figure God helped his parents train him to use that incredible strength and courage, and, most importantly, how to follow God's teaching. Each day of Samson's life was preparing him for those big adventures ahead. And later, when he grew up, he whupped some of the nastiness out of those Philistines!

God never sends us into situations without giving us the skills to handle them. Would it surprise you that God has given you incredible abilities just like Samson's? No kidding! Okay, most of us won't be running around the block with long hair and juggling small cars. Strength may not be in our godly gift pack. But never fear, we all have God-given talents. We can be good at athletics, art, music, science, computers, telling stories (ahem, that's me)— there's an entire world full of possibilities out there.

Although our gifts are different, we all have one thing in common. We have to learn how to use them the way God wants us to and keep trusting in God. We have to train and be the best we can be. To help us, God gives us parents, teachers, grandparents, ministers, and coaches. Like Sam's parents, they are all part of our success team. God doesn't want us to go it alone!

If God has done all that for us, what do we do? That's the simplest part! We learn our lessons well, try our best, and follow the good examples we find

JOKE

What are the strongest animals in the ocean?

Mussels.

in people around us and in the Bible. We can do this by learning about God, taking our schoolwork seriously, and practicing our talents.

What if you don't know what your talents are yet? That's okay, God will show them to you when the time is right, and He will give you opportunities to use them. So always be open to new things, because you never know what doors God wants you to walk through.

The next time someone suggests you try out for the solo in the church choir, sign up for a new sports team, or try a new art class, give it a try. You might be amazed at how well you do and what doors God is opening. Everybody has God-given talents, and it isn't an impossible mission to discover them and use them. All you really have

to do is your best, and let God take care of the rest. So, get out there and flex a little talent around, and be a godly example and inspiration to others!

QUESTION CORNER

* What do you think really made Samson special?
* Why shouldn't you put all your trust in your talent alone?
* What should you trust?

Samuel Listens

"Samuel grew up, and the Lord was with him and didn't let any of Samuel's words go unfulfilled" (1 Samuel 3:19).

If you think you're too young to really make a difference in the world—think again. Take the case of young Samuel! His walk with God started when he was really small.

A young wife named Hannah was very unhappy that she didn't have a baby yet. One day she was weeping and praying in God's temple. *"And she made a vow and said, 'Lord of heaven's armies, if You will look on the suffering of Your servant and remember me, and not forget Your servant, but will give me a son, then I will give him to the Lord all the days of his life"* (1 Samuel 1:11). Wow, now that's really something!

A priest named Eli was watching Hannah and went over to talk to her. She was so overcome with tears and focused on her praying that the old priest thought she was drunk! We're talking intense! She quickly explained her problem. *"Eli answered, 'Go in peace, and the God of Israel will give you what you asked Him for'"* (1 Samuel 1:17).

Hannah found joy in a bundle of joy God gave her named Samuel. She didn't forget her promise to God, though, and when Samuel was around three years old, she presented him to Eli the priest. Eli agreed to raise Samuel and promised to teach him how to serve God for the rest of his life.

Three years old may seem like a pint-sized priest in training, but it was very common in those days for the training to start when the children were very young. It must have been a strange new world for Sammy, being raised by priestly men and their families. His jobs probably included simple chores, such as sweeping and cleaning the temple, and maybe feeding animals. Samuel may have also run simple errands, like delivering messages and gophering—you know, "go fer" this and "go fer" that. He no doubt had regular lessons from the priests too.

Each year Hannah visited her son and brought him a new robe to wear. He

DIDYAKNOW?
When Jesus was twelve years old, He was in the temple in Jerusalem asking the teachers questions and giving them amazing answers.

grew up to be a good boy and learned his lessons well. He impressed everyone who knew him, and God was very proud of him.

Eli may have been a good teacher to Samuel, but his own sons used their priestly positions to take advantage of people and do evil things. Eli heard about his sons' wicked deeds, but didn't do much about it. Even after warnings from God, Eli could not change his sons' evil ways.

God rarely talked directly to people, so this made what happened to our twelve-year-old Sam even more amazing. One night, old Eli and young Samuel were sleeping in their usual spots in the holy temple just outside the inner chamber where the ark of the covenant was kept.

"The Lord called to Samuel, and he answered, 'Here I am.' And he ran to Eli and said, 'Here I am. You called me.' And Eli said, 'I didn't call. Lie down again.' So he went and lay down" (1 Samuel 3:4–5). Now, Samuel had never heard God before, so this was all very new and strange. God called Samuel three times, and each time the boy thought it was his teacher Eli.

"Then Eli realized that the Lord had called to the child. So Eli said to Samuel, 'Go, lie down. And if He calls you, then you are to say, "Speak, Lord, because Your servant is listening"'" (1 Samuel 3:8–9).

Samuel did as he was told. *"The Lord said to Samuel, 'Look, I will do something in Israel, and everyone who hears*

JOKE

Why did the boy write numbers all over his clothes? *He wanted his parents to be able to count on him.*

35

about it will be shocked. At that time I will do in full everything against Eli that I have said about his family. For I told him that I would judge his family forever for the sins he knew about. His sons dishonored God, but he didn't stop them. This is why I have told Eli's family that the guilt of Eli's family will never be wiped out by sacrifice or offering'" (1 Samuel 3:11–14).

TRIVIA

What article of clothing did the Hebrews remove before entering a home? *Shoes.*

The next morning Samuel was frightened to tell Eli what had happened, but the old priest asked for the truth, so Samuel told him all that God had said. Eli understood and accepted God's words even though the messenger was only a boy.

Samuel was some special kid, and as he grew older God continued to bless him, and made him a young man whom people respected and trusted. *"The Lord appeared again in Shiloh, for the Lord revealed Himself to Samuel in Shiloh by the word of the Lord. And the word of Samuel came to all Israel"* (1 Samuel 3:21–4:1). In time Samuel became a great prophet. A prophet was someone to whom God gave His words and who in turn gave God's words to the people. Prophets did a lot of public speaking!

There, you see? Age isn't the important thing with God. God uses people who do right things and love Him with all their heart. So if you think you have to be older before you can start working for God, you're absolutely wrong. In fact you can start right now with the little things.

Church may seem like an adult world, but it isn't. Church is your world

too! God has a spot reserved just for you! So, people, please move over and give this kid some room!

Your prayer is just as important to God as anyone else's. Really! God's paging you, so go join God's personal chat line! If you're nervous about praying out loud because you don't know any long words and you're not completely sure what to say, no problem! Long words and fast talking don't mean a thing to God. He looks into our hearts. Don't be afraid to pray for someone in church, or talk to your minister if you think God has given you something important to say. Remember, Samuel was just a kid too. God will help you find the right words or prayers that could make a difference in someone's life. So get involved! God and the adults in your life want to hear what you have to say.

QUESTION CORNER

- You may not hear voices in the middle of the night, but God is still talking with you. How does He do that?
- How can you be like Samuel?
- How can you get more involved in your church?

David the Hero

"The Lord doesn't see as people see. For people look at the outer appearance, but the Lord looks at the heart" (1 Samuel 16:7).

When it comes to kid heroes in the Bible, David has to rank in the top three spots. The guy had a throw like a baseball superstar! But that's not all, he had courage and spunk, and most importantly he had God on his team.

God put King Saul on the throne of Israel, but over time he became vain and self-important. This made God very unhappy, so He told His faithful prophet Samuel, who by this time was all grown up, to go to the small village of Bethlehem and talk to a simple shepherd named Jesse. God had chosen one of Jesse's eight sons to be the next ruler of Israel. Sssh, don't tell King Saul.

Jesse presented each of his seven older sons to the famous prophet. They were a fine, strong, handsome bunch. Any one of them looked kingly enough, but God cautioned Samuel not to judge by outward looks but rather by the heart. Samuel decided none of these sons seemed quite right. There was one more son, a boy tending his father's sheep, but Samuel asked to see him anyway.

One look told Samuel that David was just right! *"Samuel took the horn of oil and poured oil on him in front of his brothers, and the Spirit of the Lord came upon David from that day on"* (1 Samuel 16:13). God and Samuel knew that David would be king, but now it was up to God to make it happen.

In the meantime, trouble was heading toward Israel in a giant-sized way. The Philistines (remember them?) were at it again and had gathered their army for a fight with Israel. The armies made camp on opposite hillsides.

Each day this really big Philistine soldier from Gath would walk out of the enemy's camp and stand in the valley. This was not a guy you wanted to mess around with: he was nine feet tall, his helmet and armor weighed 125 pounds, and he carried a huge spear that could down an elephant. The spear alone weighed fifteen pounds! This was one

DIDYAKNOW?
Archaeologists have found sling stones that were as large as baseballs.

huge fighting machine. Man, even this guy's name was scary—Goliath.

Each day for forty days, this walking, talking mountain would shout at the Israelite soldiers, *"Why have you come out in battle formation? Am I not a Philistine, and are you not servants of Saul? Pick a man for your side, and let him come down to me. If he's able to fight with me and kill me, then we will be your servants; but if I am able to kill him, then you will be our servants and serve us"* (1 Samuel 17:8–9). Needless to say, there weren't a whole lot of volunteers for the job.

One day teenage David was in the battle camp bringing his brothers food from home. David wandered up to the front lines to chat with his brothers and the other soldiers. Then Goliath came out to tease the Israelites. David was disgusted that this big bullying Philistine should make fun of the army of God, and said so, even though his brothers basically told him to go home and shut up.

David's words were brought to King Saul's attention, and then he was brought to the king's tent. Did this worry David? Not at all! He said to the king, *"Let no man be discouraged because of him. Your servant will go and fight with this Philistine"* (1 Samuel 17:32). The king couldn't believe this boy actually wanted to fight a giant who had Israel's entire army shaking in their sandals.

But David persisted and told the king stories of how he, with God's help, had killed bears and lions while tending his father's sheep. As far as David was

DIDYAKNOW?

Robert Wadlow was the tallest man in medical history. At age ten he was already over six feet tall.

concerned, Goliath was just another bear (and he looked like one too). David explained that God had saved him from the wild animals and would also protect him from Goliath. I think the king and the older warriors all thought, "Nice kid, too bad he's going to die today." But Saul agreed to let David fight Goliath.

The king offered David his own suit of armor, but instead David took his shepherd's staff, five smooth stones from a stream, and his sling. Well, at least he'd be light on his feet.

Well, big ol' Goliath took one look at the boy "sort-of-warrior" and his shepherd's staff, and immediately got an attitude. *"Am I a dog, that you are coming against me with sticks?"* (1 Samuel 17:43).

Then he threatened to do all sorts of nasty things to David.

Did this worry our Davy? Not in the least. He replied, *"You are coming against me with a sword, a spear, and a knife. But I am coming against you in the name of the Lord of heaven's armies, the God of the armies of Israel, whom you have mocked. Today the Lord will give you into my hands. I will kill you and cut off your head . . . so that the whole world will know that there is a God in Israel"* (1 Samuel 17:45–46). David was the only one who understood the most important part of this situation—God would win the battle for him.

As battles go, this was not going to be a long one. Goliath moved closer and so did David. David quickly placed one of his stones into his leather sling and let it fly. What a shot! The stone sank into

Goliath's forehead and the giant fell like a ten-ton tree. David killed him, and before the Israelites could say, "What do you know? The kid really did it!" the Philistine army was running away.

Well, that was an amazing, courageous start to an exciting life's journey that would take David to the throne of Israel. David trusted God and used the skills He had given him, and he had faith that God would protect him. That's courage and bravery of a very special kind.

Problems or battles today don't come in the nine-foot giant variety, but we do have our own giants to face. Courage also comes in all kinds of different forms and situations. Sometimes it takes courage to tell your school or neighborhood friends that you are a Christian because you worry they will tease you or won't understand you. It takes courage to tell your school friends that when they swear and use the Lord's name in a disrespectful manner it upsets you. Or maybe dishonesty or harboring hard feelings are your giants. If you don't face them, they just get bigger. When you stand up and honor God in your daily life, you are doing exactly what David would have done. Be a hero for God in all of life's big and little situations.

QUESTION CORNER

- What was the real difference between David and Goliath as warriors?
- Who would you want on your side in a fight—a giant or a kid with faith? Why?
- What daily giants are you facing?

A Wise Choice

"Who is wise and discerning among you? Let him show his works by good conduct with wisdom's gentleness" (James 3:13).

If you could have anything in the world given to you, what would you choose? Many of us would ask for money, fame, success, or long life. But is that wise? Let's see what a young king named Solomon asked for.

King David was a very old man when a problem arose. Adonijah, David's eldest son, wanted to be king of Israel after his dad. He didn't want to wait for David to decide, so he named himself king and threw a big party. He was creating quite a royal ruckus! Now a wise prophet named Nathan understood that God, not a man, makes kings. He knew that King David's son Solomon should be king.

So King David and Nathan anointed Solomon as king and placed him on his father's mule. (Before you start to laugh, mules were considered very cool—the limousines of their day.) Solomon rode through the streets. *"They blew the trumpet; and all the people shouted, 'Long live King Solomon!' All the people followed him, playing flutes and rejoicing with great joy so that the ground shook with their sound"* (1 Kings 1:39–40). Big oops! Adonijah's

DIDYAKNOW?

In Solomon's time they considered mules to be a royal animal. A mule is a cross between a donkey and a horse.

party was over. Solomon was truly the rightful king of Israel.

Learning to be a king isn't an easy job. Before King David died, he encouraged Solomon to follow all of God's laws because that would give him a prosperous life and make him a good king.

Wouldn't that be a scary thing to have to do? Imagine that suddenly one day you have an entire room, an entire city, an entire country of adults looking to you for answers and decisions on important issues. Who, me? Yes, you! That's exactly what happened when Solomon became king. Suddenly he was expected to be smart, brave, strong, and a fair judge on all sorts of problems. I don't know about you, but all that pressure would give me a huge case of the nerves. Unfortunately there were no self-help books on being king.

"The Lord appeared to Solomon in a dream during the night. God said, 'Ask for whatever you want Me to give you.'

"Then Solomon said, 'You have shown great mercy to Your servant David, my father, because he walked before You in truth, righteousness, and integrity of heart. . . . And now, O Lord my God, You have made Your servant king in place of David my father. But I am like a little child who doesn't know how to go out or come in. And Your servant is among Your people You have chosen—so many people that they cannot be numbered or counted. Therefore give Your servant an understanding heart to judge Your people, so that I can tell the difference between good and bad. For who is able to judge this great

JOKE

How much do you have to know to teach a mule tricks? *More than the mule.*

people of Yours?'" (1 Kings 3:5–9).

Sounds like he was already pretty wise! Solomon's request for the simple gift of wisdom pleased God. *"Because you have asked for this—and have not asked for long life or riches for yourself, or for the lives of your enemies, but have asked for yourself understanding to know what is right—I now do what you requested. I give you such a wise and understanding heart that there was no one like you before, and no one like you will come after you. And I will also give you what you have not asked for: both riches and honor. During your life there will not be any like you among the kings"* (1 Kings 3:11–13).

One day, two women and one baby were brought before Solomon. I figure it was God's idea. Both women claimed to be the baby's mother. They began to fight and argue. Which one was the real mother? Nobody in the kingdom seemed to know the truth. It was plain to everyone in court that one of the women must be lying, but which one?

"*The king said, 'Bring me a sword.' So they brought a sword to the king. And the king said, 'Cut the living child in two, and give half to one and half to the other.'*

"*Then the woman whose son was alive spoke to the king, for her heart was full of love for her son. She said, 'Please, my lord, give her the living child, and don't kill him.'*

"*But the other said, 'He should not be mine or yours. Cut him in two!'*

"*Then the king answered, 'Give the living child to the first woman and don't kill him. She is his mother'*" (1 Kings 3:24–27). Pretty drastic, but he really cut through all the lies! Pretty smart guy that King Solomon, wouldn't you say? Everyone was amazed by his wisdom, and news of this great king spread to other lands.

Solomon did many good and wise things for his people and kingdom. He also built a grand and beautiful temple for the Lord in Jerusalem. Under his rule Israel was peaceful and prosperous, and Jerusalem became a famous city of learning. Solomon may have been nervous at first, but he was one straight-shooting sovereign.

DIDYAKNOW?

It took seven years to complete Solomon's temple.

What can we learn from Solomon? Solomon wasn't thinking about his own personal good or fame when he answered God. He had a real concern for his people and how he could serve them best. That wise choice and giving attitude is what pleased God.

When you pray, is your time with God completely concerned with what God can give you? God is positively *not* the genie in the magic lamp who is there to grant you new bikes, more friends, and other assorted goodies. Your time with God should never be just a wish list of wants. Want-a-mania is very uncool.

A nice way to start your prayer would be with a thank-you list of all the great things God has done for you.

Are there people in your life who can use some prayer because they are going through hard or challenging times? Ask God how you can help others around you. God does care, and He wants to help you with your dreams, goals, and needs, but don't make that the focus of every minute of your quiet time together. When you stop thinking about yourself and focus on helping and serving others, God will change your life for the better. Doing what pleases God is just the wise way to live life!

QUESTION CORNER

- Why did God give Solomon more than he prayed for?
- What would you have asked God for? Why?
- Why is wisdom such a valuable gift?

Small Words, Big Results

"As a result of the sterling character of this service, they will glorify God" (2 Corinthians 9:13).

Many times in the Bible, people were living ordinary lives when suddenly God changed things and used them to reveal His power to others. This is truly the case for a young Israelite girl. Here's what happened.

A band of men from the neighboring kingdom of Aram had crossed into the land of the Israelites. They stumbled across a young girl (perhaps a shepherdess) and took her back to Aram. Let's call her Martha.

It must have been very frightening to be swept up, carried off, and sold as a slave in a strange land. But Martha had no choice, and soon she became a good servant to the wife of a very important person. Who was this person?

"Naaman, the army commander of the king of Aram, was an important man to his master, and respected by him. . . . He was a mighty warrior" (2 Kings 5:1).

Naaman probably had no fear when he faced big, tough, drooling enemies on the battlefield, but there was one very small enemy he couldn't defeat. Naaman had a sickness called leprosy. Leprosy is caused by a small microscopic germ, or bacillus, that infects a person's skin and nerves. In those days there was no cure, and it was a terribly painful disease.

The great warrior Naaman was completely helpless, and his future looked very bleak. Hold on—Martha to the rescue! She said to her mistress, *"If only my master were with the prophet who is in Samaria! Then he would heal him of his skin disease"* (2 Kings 5:3). The prophet she was talking about was a man named Elisha who lived in Israel. Elisha was a man who knew God's heart and was famous, among other things, for how God helped him heal people.

Well, a big-time general couldn't just walk into another man's kingdom any time he liked. That would cause big problems and maybe even war, so Naaman told his king what the servant girl had said. Imagine little Martha's advice being passed on to the king!

JOKE

What do you tell a germ when it goofs around?

Don't bacilli!

"The king of Aram said, 'Go! I will send a letter to the king of Israel.' So he left and took 750 pounds of silver with him, 6,000 pieces of gold, and 10 changes of clothes. Then he brought the letter to the king of Israel, and it read: 'When you get this letter, know that I have sent my servant Naaman to you, so you can heal him of his skin disease'" (2 Kings 5:5–6).

DIDYAKNOW?

The name Elisha in Hebrew means "God is deliverance."

The king of Israel wasn't very happy about the note. In fact he got so upset that he ripped his clothes apart when he read it. Talk about a tear-rible temper! As far as he was concerned, you might as well have asked him to fly Naaman to the moon! He didn't know how to cure skin diseases. Did the king of Aram send him an impossible task just to start a fight?

The prophet Elisha heard about the situation and sent a note to the king of Israel. *"Why did you tear your clothes? Let him come to me, and he will know there is a prophet in Israel"* (2 Kings 5:8).

So Naaman went to Elisha's house in all the splendor of an important general. He probably rolled into the front yard with many servants, fine horses, and impressive chariots. What a parade! Did this impress Elisha? Not in the least. In fact he didn't even go outside! He sent a note out to the great commander telling him to go wash himself seven times in the Jordan River. Then he would be cured from his sickness.

This wasn't the kind of treatment Naaman was used to; there was no rushing around or groveling. He couldn't even get this prophet to come out and look at him! As far as Naaman was concerned, this ill-bred Israelite had just given him a note to go jump in a lake, so to speak. A dirty one to boot! He could have washed in his own rivers back home. And they were a whole lot cleaner! Well, Naaman worked himself up into a nice general-sized rage.

"Naaman got angry and went away. He said, 'Look, I thought he would certainly come out to me and stand and call on the name of the Lord his God. Then he would wave his hand over the spot and heal the skin disease'" (2 Kings 5:11).

His servants quickly tried to smooth things over. *"If the prophet had told you to do something difficult, wouldn't you have done it? How much more then, when he told you, 'Wash, and be clean'?"* (2 Kings 5:13). They had a good point!

So back went Naaman. He did exactly as Elisha said, and his skin instantly became clear of any signs of sickness. *"He returned to the man of God—he and all his group—and came and stood before him. He exclaimed, 'Now I know there is no God in all the earth except in Israel'"* (2 Kings 5:15).

TRIVIA

When you sneeze, how fast is the spray? *100 mph.*

If you were Naaman, what would you do when you got home? I'm sure he went around telling everybody about the wonders of God. And with his power and fame, people would have listened. Just think of it, a king and thousands of his subjects would hear about God for the first time because one small servant girl had the wisdom to share her faith with one person. That's incredible!

Can the same thing happen to you? Sure can! When you share your faith with someone today, you never know what an impact it may have in the future. Let's say today, over lunch at school, you share your faith with a friend. Maybe what you said doesn't seem to open her heart to the Lord. But let's flash into the future! That friend has become a president of a movie studio, or a city mayor, or state governor. One day she remembers some of the things you shared about God. She begins to follow God and has the influence to spread God's Word. Before you know it, thousands of people have a new relationship with God. Why? Because one day, over lunch, you shared your love for God. Think it's impossible? No way! God can put you in a position to change lives. One ordinary day you may have the opportunity to make an extraordinary difference. So get out there and share your faith. It changes the future for the better.

QUESTION CORNER

- What might have happened if Martha hadn't shared what she knew?
- How can you make a difference?
- What could you tell people about God?

A Healthy Dose of Healing!

You just never know when a miracle can make your day. A miracle is something extraordinary that God makes happen. We can experience miracles, but we just can't explain how they happen. God designed our world, and He can change the way it works any time He likes. Here are some amazing examples of miracles that were really "to die for." You'll see what I mean.

The kingdom of Israel had turned to evil ways, and God was very angry and decided to punish Israel with a great drought and famine. He would cause no rain or dew to fall for several years. God warned His holy man Elijah and kept him safe.

Some time later during the drought, God sent Elijah to a widow and her young son in the town of Zarephath. The widow was just coming outside the village gates to find firewood. Elijah approached her and asked for water and food. She explained that they had only enough food to make one more meal. *"Elijah said to her, 'Don't be afraid. Go and do as you said, but first make me a little loaf from it and bring it to me. After that, make one for yourself and for your son. For this is what the Lord God of Israel says: "The barrel of meal will not become empty and the jar of oil will not run dry until the day that the Lord sends rain on the ground"'"* (1 Kings 17:13–14). She must have wondered if he was rude, a thief, or just plain nuts. But there was something special about him, and she did as she was asked. Because of her trust, her little family and Elijah had food every day. All because of God's amazing, never-ending barrels and jars!

Later, the little boy got sick. Each day he felt sicker and weaker. Then one sad day he died. His mother was overcome with grief and thought Elijah the prophet was punishing her.

Elijah was a kind man and was sad for the widow and her son. *"He said to her, 'Give me your son.' And he took him from her arms, and carried him upstairs where he was staying, and laid him down*

JOKE

What sickness can't you talk about until you're cured? *Laryngitis.*

58

on his own bed. Then he cried out to the Lord: 'O Lord my God, have You brought misery on even this widow I'm staying with, by killing her son?'

And he stretched himself over the child three times and cried out to the Lord: 'O Lord my God, I pray that this child's life return to him.' And the Lord heard Elijah's voice, and the life of the child returned to him, and he lived" (1 Kings 17:19–22).

The boy probably awoke puzzled; suddenly he didn't feel sick. In fact, he felt just fine! The widow was naturally happy and amazed. *"And the woman said to Elijah, 'Now I know that you are a man of God, and that the word of the Lord in your mouth is true'"* (1 Kings 17:24). The boy probably wanted to head outside and play. Wow, what an amazing miracle! After all, a second life is a gift for, well, a lifetime!

Want to hear another great death and life story? Remember Elisha, the prophet who sent that general for a healthy dip? Well, he visited the town of Shunem so often that a kind, wealthy woman invited him and his servant Gehazi to stay with her and her husband whenever they were in town. They even made him a room with a view on the roof.

This kindly couple had no children. As a thank-you, Elisha said, *"About this time next year, you will hold a son in your arms"* (2 Kings 4:16). The woman was very surprised, but she was also frightened that if she got her hopes up

TRIVIA

What miracle did both Elijah and Elisha do at the Jordan River?

They each parted the river water so they could cross on dry land.

and the prophet was wrong, she would be bitterly disappointed. But she had no reason to worry, for just as Elisha had said, a year later she had a baby.

One day the boy was with his father in the fields when suddenly he cried out. *"'My head, my head!' Then the father said to a servant, 'Carry him to his mother'"* (2 Kings 4:19). Sadly the little boy died in his mom's arms, and she laid him on a bed. She didn't tell her husband but took a servant and a donkey to visit Elisha on Mount Carmel. When she reached Elisha, she fell to the ground and held his feet.

"Gehazi came near to push her away. However, the man of God said, 'Leave her alone; for she is bitterly upset, and the Lord has hidden it from me and has not told me about it.'

"Then she said, 'Did I ask for a son from my lord? Did I not say, "Don't deceive me?"'" (2 Kings 4:27–28). Elisha realized instantly what had happened and sent Gehazi ahead with special instructions to heal the boy. Gehazi did what he was told, but nothing happened.

"When Elisha came into the house, the boy was dead and had been laid on his bed. So he went in and shut the door behind the two of them, and prayed to the Lord. And he got up on the bed and lay on the child, putting his mouth on his mouth, his eyes on his eyes, and his hands on his hands. He stretched out over the child, and the child's flesh became warm. Then he got down, and walked back and forth in the house, and got up on the bed and stretched

DIDYAKNOW?
One of longest recorded sneezing attacks lasted 978 days. Now that's nothing to sneeze at.

himself over him. Then the boy sneezed seven times and opened his eyes" (2 Kings 4:32–35). Talk about a flat out healing!

Absolutely, positively, amazingly fantastic! How did these two very special guys do those miracles? They had complete trust that God heard their prayers, and they had special lifelong relationships with God.

But are miracles a thing of the past? NO WAY! God uses people of faith right now, today, this very minute. God could even use you! I'm not joking. God doesn't have rules on who He uses to do amazing things. If you believe in Him and have a willing heart and courage to pray for people, God can use you to bless others. Some miracles DO happen right away like the two little boys in the story, but other miracles may take months or years. God's miracles aren't like food you pop in the microwave and ten seconds later they're done. We can't predict when or how God is going to use His power. Our job is to never stop praying for others because God never stops listening and caring.

QUESTION CORNER

- Who really healed the boys?
- How many Bible miracles can you list?
- What are you praying for? Can God answer you? How do you know?

The Kid Who Would Be King

"Any day I am afraid, I will trust in You. In God—I praise is word—in God I trust. I will not fear what anyone can do to me" (Psalm 56:3–4).

It is easy to trust God when our lives are happy and content. But what about when we face tough situations? Who do we turn to for help? When trouble comes into our lives, do we have the faith to let God take control, or do we try to fix things ourselves? Here's a story of a young king who lost faith and tried to go it alone. Did it work out? I'll let you be the judge.

The baby prince Joash started out life in the middle of great danger and evil. His father King Ahaziah died, and before the dust could settle, his grandmother Athaliah took over and made herself queen. She decided to destroy anything that would keep her from the throne—that included killing her grandchildren. Not exactly a grandmother you want to share milk and cookies with, is she?

DIDYAKNOW?

One of the largest piles of coins ever made contained three million.

Joash's aunt was frightened that Queen Athaliah would kill him, so Auntie Jehosheba hid Joash and later left him with the high priest Jehoiada. Prince Joash's secret royal training began! They hid Joash from his grandmother for six years.

When Joash was seven years old, the high priest decided the young prince was ready to take the throne. Do you think you could be king at seven? Scary, huh. Jehoiada gathered a small army of loyal guards. They were about to do a very daring thing. Protecting the young prince, they took him to the temple. *"The guards stood, every one with his weapons in his hand, around the king, from the right side of the temple to the left side, at the altar and at the temple"* (2 Kings 11:11). Then before anybody could stop them, *"Jehoiada brought out the king's son, put the crown on him, and gave him a copy of the covenant. They made him king, poured oil on him, and clapped their hands, saying, 'Long live the king!'"* (2 Kings 11:12).

It took seven years to make it happen, but the true king was on his rightful throne at long last, and the people of Israel were glad. As for his wicked grandmother? There was nothing she could do

about it. And that was the end of her!

With the help of the faithful high priest Jehoiada, little Joash grew and became a good king. Joash always followed the priest's wise advice. *"Joash did what was right in the sight of the Lord all his life, as Jehoiada the priest instructed him"* (2 Kings 12:2). All's well that ends well! Right? Weeell, we'll see.

During his rule, Joash started a project to restore the aging temple that Solomon had built. It seems Joash was a good money manager of this project, for soon the building was full of workmen. *"They gave the money that was weighed to the men in charge of the work on the temple of the Lord. They, in turn, paid the carpenters*

JOKE
What kind of party did Joash throw for Hazael?
A going-away party.

and builders who worked on the temple of the Lord. They also paid the stoneworkers and the stonecutters. They bought wood and cut stone to make repairs on the temple of the Lord. And they paid for everything else needed to repair the temple" (2 Kings 12:11–12).

Everything was going great, and the temple was restored to its earlier brilliance. Joash was a contented king. But, sadly, good Jehoiada died, and king Joash started listening to some bad advice. It seems our boy king never learned to tell right from wrong on his own. He even turned away from God. Big mistake . . . no, huge mistake!

Don't get too comfortable, Joash, because Hazael the king of Aram is up to no good. (Do you think this was one way for God to test Joash's faith? Let's find out.) Hazael's army was attacking and capturing cities right, left, and center. And now he had his eye on Jerusalem. When Joash heard the news, he became a very, very nervous king. He couldn't see any way of stopping Hazael. What did he do? Well, I think he got so scared that he wasn't even thinking straight. He certainly never stopped to pray to God for a solution to the problem. Instead, he rushed into the palace and God's temple and collected all the gold he could jimmy off the walls or stuff in a sack. Then he gave that bully Hazael every ounce of God's treasure. And he didn't even stop to ask God if he could! After giving King Hazael all that loot, Joash begged him to go away. Hazael was more than glad to get paid off, so he left Joash and Jerusalem alone.

Now, how do you think God felt when Joash didn't even consult Him, and then proceeded to trash His holy temple? I would guess completely unimpressed. After that, it seems things didn't go too well for our young king. God no longer gave Joash His blessing. King Joash faced trouble upon trouble the rest of his life.

You see, the big problem was that Jehoiada's faith and teaching were the only things keeping Joash on the right path. Joash never learned to love and follow God on his own. Following God has to be your own personal choice. You can't have a relationship with God through your parents or friends. YOU have to want God in your life because YOU want to follow Him.

DIDYAKNOW?

The temple's treasure house in Jerusalem was known to contain as much as 50 tons of stored gold.

The other problem was that Joash didn't have enough faith or respect in God to allow Him to take control of the situation. Joash relied on his own earthly knowledge to solve the problem, and he didn't even seem to care if it was the right thing to do. He never found that special courage that comes from believing in God's protection.

Do you sometimes forget to talk to God and trust Him when times get scary and tough? God is our wise counselor and protector. He can, will, and does help us with our earthly problems because He's our heavenly Father, and fathers look after their children. We all get into situations that make us nervous or even afraid. You know, like if you get lost in a busy place, or the school bully has decided to pay you a not-so-welcome visit on the playground. Just send up an SOS to your heavenly Father and He'll go into action. He may not handle the situation the way you would, but if you have the problem, God's got the solution.

QUESTION CORNER

- Why do you think Joash turned away from God after Jehoiada died?
- Who do you turn to in times of trouble?
- Whose advice do you take? Why?

Josiah and the Clean Sweep

"You have treated Your servant well, as You promised in Your word, O Lord. Teach me good sense and knowledge, for I rely on your commandments" (Psalm 119:65–66).

Have you ever been someplace and suddenly had the feeling that something was very wrong? Why does that happen? We know what feels right from wrong because we have experience or understanding of what IS right or normal. That's called knowledge. Here's a story about a young king who got a sudden blast of godly knowledge and instantly knew things were terribly wrong.

Josiah was only eight years old

when he became king of Israel, and for a child king he did better than some adults. But something very important was missing from his education.

After Josiah had been king for a few years, he ordered repair work to be done on the temple. One day when his secretary Shaphan was at the temple on some renovation business, the high priest Hilkiah came to him with a long-lost discovery. (Well, blow the dust off and let's all have a look!) *"I have found a scroll of the law in the temple of the Lord.' And Hilkiah gave the scroll to Shaphan, and he read it. And Shaphan the scribe came to the king, and brought a report to him"* (2 Kings 22:8–9). The book apparently had been missing for a very long

time—maybe since Joash's time or longer. If it had been a library book, they would have been in for one huge overdue fine. But then maybe God thought this literary find was long overdue.

The book they found may have been the book of Deuteronomy written by our old pal Moses. (Hey, we're talking old!) This book contains the rules and laws given to Israel by God. That seems like an awfully important book to be missing. *"When the king heard the words of the scroll of the law, he tore his clothes"* (2 Kings 22:11). (Wow, these kings are really hard on their clothes!)

Remember having the knowledge of right and wrong? Well, poor Josiah just got an eye-opener. Suddenly he had that terrible sinking feeling that things were very wrong in his kingdom. If only he had known before!

What did Josiah realize? People had forgotten about God. This wasn't completely his fault. You see, before Josiah there were a number of bad kings who had worshiped false gods and allowed sinful activities to grow in the kingdom. Josiah had grown up with these wrong ideas and hadn't realized that they were all terrible insults to God. But now he understood and was shocked and saddened. But he was also ready to do something about it! (Go get 'em, Josiah.) The first thing he did was to ask his counselors to pray to God for His understanding about the book they found and to reveal His heart to them. Smart move!

Hilkiah the high priest and some of Josiah's other trusted men went to a holy woman named Huldah, who was a prophetess. (Get ready for a lecture, men; after all, you deserve it.) She told them what the Lord said, *"I am going to bring disaster on this place and on its people, as predicted in the words of the scroll that the king of Judah read. Because they have left Me and have burned incense to other gods, provoking Me to anger by everything they did, My anger will burn against this place and will not be put out"* (2 Kings 22:16–17).

It was clear that God was angry, but He was also pleased that Josiah had been shocked and saddened by the state of his kingdom, that he had humbled himself before the Lord, and that he had a willing heart to do what was right. So God promised not to punish Israel for their wicked ways until Josiah was dead.

Whew, what a relief. But Josiah wasn't just going to leave it at that. Time to clean house! The next right thing that Josiah did was to gather absolutely everybody in the kingdom to the temple. *"The king stood by the pillar and made a covenant in the presence of the Lord. He promised to follow the Lord and to keep His commandments, testimonies, and statutes with all his heart and soul. He agreed to practice the words of this covenant that were written in this scroll. And all the people promised to obey the covenant"* (2 Kings 23:3).

Now it was time to make a clean sweep, so to speak. Josiah removed from the temple all the things the people used to worship false gods, and sent their evil priests packing. Then Josiah swept through the kingdom removing evil things and evil people. Also, *"The king commanded all the people, saying, 'Celebrate the Passover to the Lord your God, as it is written in this scroll of the covenant'"* (2 Kings 23:21). All of Israel did as their king commanded.

Finally, Josiah felt right and good about all that he had done and the changes he had made. God was very pleased. *"Never before was there a king like him who turned to the Lord with all his heart, all his soul, and all his might, according to the law of Moses. Never again was there a king like him"* (2 Kings 23:25).

The first important thing to know is this—not knowing the rules for right

DIDYAKNOW?

There are only four female prophets mentioned in the Old Testament: Miriam, Deborah, Isaiah's wife, and Huldah.

and wrong is not an excuse for doing wrong things. Those types of excuses don't work with God. You have to MAKE IT your business to find out what God says is right or wrong. The best way to stay out of trouble is to educate yourself on what IS trouble. Knowledge is the first defense against temptation, doing wrong things, and disappointing God. So get in the know! You get godly knowledge the same way Josiah did, by reading the Bible.

If we do something absolutely wrong, like stealing candy from a store or telling a lie, we have to be brave enough to clean shop too. We have to take our mistake to God and ask for His forgiveness and advice. Then we have to do the same to the people we hurt. And then comes the hard part—correcting our mistakes. Maybe we have to go to that store and really clean shop to pay for the item we took. Being wrong isn't nice or fun, but we can learn from our mistakes, change our ways, and become better people because of them. Godly knowledge is the key to knowing right, believing right, and doing right.

QUESTION CORNER

☀ Why do you think Josiah was so upset when he read the book?
☀ If you read God's laws for the first time, what would you do?
☀ What kind of changes in your life would you make?

Prepared Messenger

"Be ready for service and have your lamps lit" (Luke 12:35).

Ready or not, God's going to dust you off, point you in the right direction, and get you started on the wonderful adventure called your life. Sounds great, but there's one little problem—God's ready, but you might not be too sure you are. If you worry that you just don't have what it takes to follow God's plan, you're not alone. There's a whole list of uncertain adventurers in the Bible. Take the case of Jeremiah. He certainly didn't start off

75

with oodles of confidence.

Jeremiah was the son of Hilkiah the high priest in the troubled court of King Josiah. Anyway, when Jeremiah was a teenager, something truly amazing happened—God personally told Jeremiah about the plan for his life.

"The word of the Lord came to me: 'Before I formed you within your mother's body, I knew you, and before you were born, I set you apart, and I appointed you to be a prophet to the nations'" (Jeremiah 1:4–5). God certainly gave Jerry a prophetable plan! How could he say no?

What was Jeremiah's response to this startling news? *"Then I said, 'Ah, Lord God! I really don't know how to speak,*

DIDYAKNOW?
There are about 773,700 words in an English Bible, and an average of 3,566,480 letters!

for I am a child'" (Jeremiah 1:6). Actually age is never a good excuse to get out of godly achievements. Clearly, Jerry had a sudden case of the nerves and a huge dose of self-doubt; after all, being God's prophet to entire nations was a big, big job. But it's okay to be nervous! God understood Jeremiah's reluctance.

"The Lord said to me, 'Don't say, "I am a child," for you are to go to everyone I send you to and say everything I command you. Don't be afraid of them, for I am with you to rescue you,' says the Lord" (Jeremiah 1:7–8). (See, I told you the age excuse doesn't work.) The thing Jerry's got to realize is, with God backing you up, who's going to knock you down?

Our own fears can be the number one roadblock in our walk with God. In fact, God wants us to be confident that He's with us every step of the way! (I

mean, I was worried I'd get left on the shelf. But here we are! So relax!) God is always prepared and He makes sure we have the proper equipment!

What are the tools of the trade for a prophet? Well, prophets do a lot of talking and counseling to kings and other important people, so God gave Jeremiah just what he needed.

"The Lord put out His hand and touched my mouth. Then the Lord said to me, 'There! I have put My words in your mouth. Look, today I have appointed you over the nations and over the kingdoms, to uproot and to tear down, to destroy and to demolish, to build and to plant'" (Jeremiah 1:9–10). Zikes! Talk about an earthshaking job descrip-tion! I don't think you can learn that kind of stuff at school. Jerry's in God's class now.

You can't use a tool unless you know how it works, so God gave Jeremiah a quick lesson on how to use his gift of visions and words.

"The word of the Lord came to me: 'What do you see, Jeremiah?'

"And I said, 'I see a branch of an almond tree.'

"Then the Lord said to me, 'You have seen right: for I am watching over My word to carry it out'" (Jeremiah 1:11–12). Yeah, way to go Jer! He got his first lesson right.

You see, God was carefully planting the seeds of courage, confidence, and ability in Jeremiah that night. Now it was time to reveal what the adventure was going to be. *"The word of the Lord came to me a second time: 'What do you see?'*

"And I said, 'I see a boiling pot tipping over from the north.'

"Then the Lord said to me, 'Disaster will be poured out against all the people of this land. For I am about to call all the people of the northern kingdoms,' says the Lord. 'They will come, and each one will place his throne at the entrance of the gates of Jerusalem, and against all the walls around her, and against all the cities of Judah. And I will announce My judgments against them because of all their wickedness. They have left Me, have burned incense to other gods, and have worshiped idols they made with their own hands'" (Jeremiah 1:13–16).

God had chosen Jeremiah to warn the kingdom that hardship and sadness was coming because of their wicked ways. As you might have guessed, Jeremiah was a little concerned. He was just a kid! How could he possibly tell great and powerful men this terrible news! They'd get mad, they'd yell, they'd throw him in jail . . . or worse. He felt he just wasn't ready for this job. Ah, but God knew he was. Jeremiah got the fatherly shove out the door that he needed.

"But you, get ready. Stand up and tell them everything that I command you. Don't be discouraged by them or else I will discourage you in front of them. Look, today I have made you like a fortified city, like an iron pillar, and like walls of bronze against the whole land, against the kings of Judah, its princes, its priests, and the people of the land" (Jeremiah 1:17–18).

TRIVIA

Was Jeremiah known as a prophet or a patriarch? *Prophet.*

Those are JUST the words of encouragement Jeremiah needed. Now, he was ready to be God's man and follow the plan God had for him.

Are you as ready as Jeremiah, or do you get stuck at square one because you're too afraid to trust God? Good question. God has a plan and purpose for each of us, but He has also given us the choice to follow His plan or go our own way. When we come to those big decisions in our walk with God, remember Jeremiah and the four things God did for him: 1) Promised to protect and guide him; 2) Gave him the abilities to succeed; 3) Taught him how to use those abilities; and 4) Revealed exactly what He expected Jeremiah to do.

God will do everything to prepare you for your life's purpose. So the next time God asks you to do something you've never done before, go ahead and do it. Be ready, be confident, be bold, be adventurous, be the person God knows you can be!

QUESTION CORNER

* How can God already have a plan for you before you are even born?
* What lessons has God been teaching you to prepare you for His plan?
* How can you overcome your own nervousness?

What a Team!
Daniel, Shadrach, Meshach, and Abednego

"My steps hold fast on Your paths, my feet have not slipped" (Psalm 17:5).

We all face adversity in different ways. What is adversity? It's an experience of the not-so-nice kind. When we face conflicts, suffering, or disasters, we are looking adversity in the eye. Whether we sink under the waves of a problem like a sinking Titanic or surf through the situation on a sleek board of godly confidence will directly depend on our trust and commitment to God. Here's the story of four very determined and surfing guys.

Adversity came to Judah in the form of a big, bad Babylonian king with a really long name. King Nebuchadnezzar attacked and took over Judah just as God had said he would. This king had one of those Babylonian not-so-great ideas! He decided to take young men from the royal and noble families of Judah and raise them as Babylonians. He wanted the best of the best! They had to be very smart, handsome, and athletic. It seems the king wanted them taught the language and literature of his people. The young men would be given new names and would live, eat, and learn to do all things like true Babylonians.

"The king allotted for them a daily amount of the king's provisions and the wine that he drank. They were to be trained for three years and at the end of that time they were to serve in the king's court" (Daniel 1:5).

ENTER our four brave guys: Daniel, Hananiah, Mishael, and Azariah. They didn't like this idea of Babylonian re-education. They didn't want new Babylonian names (Belteshazzar, Shadrach, Meshach, and Abednego), they didn't want to eat their unholy food, and they certainly didn't want to worship any false gods. But what could they do? If they didn't cooperate, they would likely be killed. These four guys formed a team to remain strong and true to their God no matter what. I think their motto could have been "One for all and all for God!"

Daniel was the first to suggest that they try to bend the rules in their favor.

DIDYAKNOW?

A brain cell has the longest life of any cell? It will last a lifetime.

The boys didn't want to eat food or drink wine that might have been offered to idols, prepared in an unholy manner, or was forbidden by the Law of Moses. After all, you are what you eat! Daniel asked the chief official taking care of them to allow them to eat only vegetables. The guard had his doubts, *"My lord the king allotted your food and your drink. I'm afraid of what would happen if he saw your faces looking thinner than the young men who are your age. You would have put my head in danger with the king"* (Daniel 1:10). (You know, head minus body. Ouch!)

Daniel was smart and suggested that the guard test them for ten days on their veggie diet. If they looked in any way unhealthy, they'd go back to Babylonian burgers and all.

God caused the chief official to be sympathetic to Daniel and the boys, and he agreed. *"At the end of ten days their appearance was better and they were healthier than all the young men who were eating the king's provisions"* (Daniel 1:15). Way to go, guys! Daniel and his friends showed God their willingness to stay true to His laws despite all adversity.

Knowledge and wisdom can be one of the most powerful tools against overwhelming situations. Pick brain over brawn power every time. *"As for these four young men, God gave them knowledge and proficiency in all literature and wisdom. Daniel even understood all visions and dreams"* (Daniel 1:17). Why was this so important?

TRIVIA

How much smarter than the Babylonians did God make Daniel and his friends?

Ten times smarter.

The situation was soon to turn into a Babylonian battle of the brains. If the boys failed to prove to King Nebuchadnezzar that they were truly resourceful and useful to his kingdom, it could well mean their deaths. Time to tinker with the old thinkers! *"At the end of the time, when the king had said to bring them, the commander of the court officials brought them before Nebuchadnezzar. The king interviewed them, and no one was found among them like Daniel, Hananiah, Mishael, and Azariah. So they began to serve in the king's court. In every matter of wisdom and understanding about which the king consulted them, he found them ten times better than all the magicians and conjurers who were in his whole kingdom"* (Daniel 1:18–20).

Remember, God always prepares us for our battles in life. The young men managed to survive this and other very hot Babylonian ordeals without compromising their faith in God and their obedience in His laws. How? They stood firm where they could, and that takes courage when everything in your life seems to be out of your control and swamped with adversity. Sure, eating vegetables for years may not seem like a huge stand for holiness, but it showed to others and God their willingness to do the right things.

I can almost guarantee you that we will never be overrun by Babylonians, but conflicts do happen in our lives and sometimes we have to take godly stands in the face of adversity. That might mean telling your coach that you can't

> **JOKE**
>
> What vegetable should you never eat on a boat?
> *A leek.*

play on Sunday mornings because your family goes to church. Or maybe not watching the video your friend rented for your sleepover because it doesn't have good values or morals. In the big scheme of life, that may seem like a small sacrifice, but if we can't stand firm in small areas, how are we going to have the courage to be godly in the really tough situations? Little, daily, right steps add up to a lifelong walk with God.

QUESTION CORNER

* What might have happened to Daniel and company if they hadn't stood up for God? Would we have ever heard of them? Why or why not?
* Would you find it hard to take a stand for God? Why or why not?
* What challenges do you face?

Lemons or Lemonade?

"Set an example of good works yourself, with integrity and dignity in your teaching. Your message is to be sound beyond reproach, so that the opponent will be ashamed, having nothing bad to say about us" (Titus 2:7–8).

A positive attitude can make all the difference in the world. Like the old saying goes, "When you get handed a lemon, make lemonade!" In other words, make something great out of a really sour situation. Every person on this planet has encountered situations that don't seem fair, right, or even pleasant. How we deal with them can mean the difference between disaster or victory. Take the story of this orphan girl.

The Persian Empire stretched from India to Greece and into Africa. The Persian king had absolute power. Everything he said was law and had to be obeyed.

In the Persian town of Susa lived a beautiful Jewish orphan girl named Hadassah. She was loved and raised by her cousin Mordecai. They were descendants of Israelites carried off by King Nebuchadnezzar, and the Israelites still had many enemies in Persia. Hadassah didn't use her Hebrew name but was known throughout by her Persian name, Esther.

Esther loved her cousin and was very happy until one day a terrible thing happened. She was taken away from home! King Ahasuerus had ordered that all beautiful girls from across the kingdom were to be taken to his palace. Did Esther have a choice? Probably not. This was a king's law. Beautiful Esther and hundreds of other young girls were separated from their families and sent to the palace. They were like beautiful captives in a splendid palace prison. Once there they were carefully watched over and trained in palace ways by a man named Hegai.

This must have been a terrifying experience, and Esther must have been very homesick. This was one invitation she could have done without! Was it right or fair? Of course not, but that didn't change the situation. Kings rule, so they get to make the rules.

Esther could have done several things: cried all the time, been angry and

DIDYAKNOW?
Some makeup used by ancient women also worked as a fly repellent.

rude, or stayed moody and depressed. Nope, not our Esther. I think she decided to be the winner of this situation by being wise, charming, and careful. Esther most likely made a point of doing what she was told, learning her lessons, and being pleasant in all situations. At any rate, she greatly impressed her guardian Hegai.

"The young woman pleased him, and she won his favor; and he quickly gave her cosmetics and special foods. Seven young women, handpicked from the king's palace, were given to her. He transferred her and her young women to the best part of the women's quarters" (Esther 2:9). The harem was the part of the palace where the young girls lived. Smart Esther was making her own rules in this royal game.

Her cousin Mordecai was not allowed to see Esther, and he worried about her constantly. *"Every day Mordecai walked in front of the court of the women's quarters to find out how Esther was and what was happening to her"* (Esther 2:11). Would she be all right? Were they treating her fairly? And most importantly, was she keeping her secret? You see, Mordecai knew that many people in the palace hated the Hebrews, and this would not go well for Esther. So Mordecai forbade her to reveal her nationality or family background.

"Before each woman's turn came to go to King Ahasuerus, she completed twelve months of treatments prescribed for

---

DIDYAKNOW?

Bible women used crushed minerals and plants as make-up. The mineral galena was used for their eyelids, and crushed henna leaves tinted their hair, lips, cheeks, toes, and finger-nails red.

women. *The beauty treatments included six months with oil of myrrh, and six months with perfumes and other women's cosmetics*" (Esther 2:12). Talk about a beauty makeover! Esther put up with all the primping and fussing with good humor. The day was fast approaching for her to meet the king. Esther was smart and she sought the advice of Hegai on how to present herself to the king: what to say, how to act, and what to do. Hegai liked Esther and was more than happy to help.

The big day came and Esther was taken to meet the great king of Persia. Her very future depended on whether the king was pleased with her or not. This was a game she had to win.

All her hard work, planning, and good attitude paid off. What caught the king's attention? I think he was completely taken with her beauty, wit, grace, and bright personality. He put a royal crown on her head and made her his queen.

Queen Esther would later play a risky game of life or death for her people. She would match wits with a master schemer. Did God help her win? That's a story for another day.

Meanwhile back at the palace. . . .

"The king made a great feast for all his nobles and officials—called 'Esther's feast.' He gave a tax holiday to the provinces and distributed royal gifts" (Esther 2:18).

Esther certainly won that victory with style, charm, and an attitude to win. She turned a negative situation into a positive experience. When we're

put into tough situations, it is up to us to tackle them with the right attitudes. Not only will that help us succeed, but it will also be a witness to the people around us. *"Esther won the favor of everyone who saw her"* (Esther 2:15).

Let's say somebody at school accidentally damages a poster you spent weeks designing and painting. Do you scream and yell? Do you go over and wreck their poster? Do you moan and complain to your teacher? Nope. After you get over the first wave of shock and disappointment, you kindly accept that person's apology and fix your poster. Sure, maybe your poster won't be as great as before, but do you know what is even better? People notice and are impressed with your great attitude. The next time your art teacher wants an important project done, like painting a mural on the cafeteria wall, she might remember your talent, and most importantly, your mature attitude. Before you know it—you have the job. That's how God meant the world to work. So impress people with your lemonade-making skills. You'll be the winner and a good witness about God's right attitudes.

QUESTION CORNER

- What did Esther do to win favor from those over her? How can you be like Esther?
- Where and when can the right attitude pay off for you?
- What attitudes do you admire?

92

Who's Lost?

We have all heard the story of Jesus' birth in the manger in Bethlehem and later about Jesus the Man. What about the in-between times? After all, Jesus had to grow up before He became a man!

"Every year His parents traveled to Jerusalem for the Passover Festival. When He was twelve years old, they went up according to the custom of the festival" (Luke 2:41–42). The Passover was a very important Jewish holiday celebrating

how God saved and rescued their people from Egypt under Moses. The holiday lasted eight days and had a ceremonial meal called the Seder. During the Seder, special foods were served, the story of the Exodus (or exit) from Egypt was retold, and prayers of thanksgiving were offered to God.

During the Passover, households in Jerusalem would overflow with the company of out-of-town relatives and friends. This must have been an exciting time for young Jesus. He was going to Jerusalem—the biggest, busiest city in all the land! The markets would be full of merchants and exotic wares, travelers from afar would crowd

DIDYAKNOW?

Many travelers came to Jerusalem to celebrate three religious holidays: Passover, the Feast of Weeks, and the Feast of Tabernacles.

the inns, and Jesus and His family would visit friends and relatives. And most importantly, He would worship at the great temple of Jerusalem. What would it be like? For a small town kid, it meant big time adventure!

Even before He got to the city, Jesus could see the grand temple resting like a white jewel above the city on a hill. Once inside, the temple was a maze of courtyards, covered walkways, wide porches, large white colonnades of carved stone, and golden decorations. It was beautiful, but it was also a hive of exciting events. Every day thousands of people poured into the temple to worship, sacrifice offerings of small animals, and listen to the great religious thinkers and teachers of the day. Every area of the great building seemed to be overflowing with people, music, and activities. What

a wondrous place for a twelve-year-old boy named Jesus! This was a place made for exploring and watching.

"After those days were over, as they were returning, the boy Jesus stayed behind in Jerusalem, but His parents did not know it. Assuming He was in the traveling party, they went a day's journey. Then they began looking for Him among their relatives and friends" (Luke 2:43–44). Everybody must have thought Jesus was with another group of homeward-bound friends or relatives. Stop those camels and turn around those donkeys. This caravan had to make an emergency landing!

"When they did not find Him, they returned to Jerusalem to search for Him.

What question must you always answer yes to? *What does Y-E-S spell?*

After three days, they found Him in the temple complex sitting among the teachers, listening to them and asking them questions" (Luke 2:45–46).

If you or I had been lost in a great city like Jerusalem all by ourselves, we would probably have been terrified. (I was once mis-catalogued and I didn't like it a bit.) But not so for Jesus. For three days the unworried boy sat in the temple asking great men questions and discussing the Scriptures. *"All those who heard Him were astounded at His understanding and His answers"* (Luke 2:47). Apparently not half as amazed as Jesus' parents!

"When his parents saw Him, they were astonished, and His mother said to Him, 'Son, why have You treated us like this? Here Your father and I have been anxiously searching for You.'

*"'Why were you searching for Me?'
He asked them. 'Didn't you know that I
must be involved in my Father's interests?'
But they did not understand what He said
to them"* (Luke 2:48–50). But Jesus knew,
all too well. Even as a young boy, it
seems He already understood His special
relationship with His heavenly Father
and His very important purpose in life.
He seemed almost surprised that His
parents didn't see heavenly matters as
clearly as He did. Being in the temple
worshiping, talking about His Father in
heaven, must have seemed the most
natural thing in the world to Him.

*"Then He went down with them and
came to Nazareth, and was obedient to
them. His mother kept all these things in
her heart"* (Luke 2:51). Mary knew that
her boy was special beyond understanding. Soon, as Jesus grew, His uniqueness

was clear to all who met Him. *"And Jesus
increased in wisdom and
stature and in favor with
God and with people"*
(Luke 2:52).

Here's a question
to think about. Who was
really lost, Jesus or His
parents? Hmmm. Jesus,
after all, was very confident in where He was
supposed to be.

DIDYAKNOW?

Historians esti-
mate that there
could have been
three million peo-
ple in Jerusalem
during Passover.

Here's another important question.
Do we, in the hustle and bustle of our
own daily lives, find ourselves far away
from Jesus' presence? Do we suddenly
stop and wonder, "Hey, where's Jesus in
my life?" Ever wonder where He's gone
and why He's left you all alone? Well, the
simple truth is, Jesus has been in the right
place all along. He's been waiting for you

to look for Him in His Father's house. You're the one who has journeyed away and forgotten to keep in contact.

Jesus loves us and wants to have a close and loving relationship with us, but He doesn't really want to chase after us all the time. A good relationship is when both sides want to set aside time just to be with each other to talk and share stuff. Are you remembering to share your time with Jesus? Do you remember where to find Him?

Set some time aside to take a walk and discuss your day with Jesus, maybe ask Him a few questions, and certainly thank Him for the great things He is doing in your life. Ask Jesus to come live in your heart and home. He will always be your best friend, and best friends always keep in touch. So go and spend time with your Savior. We don't have to search for Jesus, because He's right there when we need Him and He's been there all the time.

QUESTION CORNER

- When Jesus was twelve, why do you think He was asking questions in the temple?
- How do you think He knew the answers He did?
- What questions about God do you have? Who can help you find the answers?

Lunch Is in the Bag!

"If the readiness is there, [the gift] is acceptable according to whatever one has, not according to what he does not have" (2 Corinthians 8:12).

Hey, did you hear about the quadruple billionaire who gave over a billion dollars to a children's charity? A billion dollars! Wow, that's one pile of cash! News like that can make us feel a little shortchanged.

We rattle around the few coins we have in our piggybanks and figure, "Hey what can my little amount do to help the world?" Well, don't give thoughts like that a chance to multiply, because God has a plan to use whatever you give for big purposes. You have plenty to contribute, even if you don't know it yet—which reminds me of the little boy (let's call him Ladan) who had one surprisingly full lunch.

Ladan had probably spent the day watching the miracles that Jesus performed on the sick. He had never seen anything like it before: crippled people were dancing and the sick were cured! This was a day he'd never forget! After a while, Ladan watched as Jesus and His followers went across the lake to the far shore. Some of the people quickly crowded into fishing boats or ran along the shore to follow them.

Ladan, swept up in the excitement and adventure of it all, followed the crowd.

"Jesus crossed the Sea of Galilee (or Tiberias). And a huge crowd was following Him because they saw the signs that He was performing on the sick. So Jesus went up a mountain and sat down there with His disciples. . . .

"When Jesus raised His eyes and noticed a huge crowd coming toward Him, He asked Philip, 'Where will we buy bread so these people can eat?' He asked this to test him, for He Himself knew what He was going to do" (John 6:1–3, 5–6).

Poor Philip took one look at this crowd of thousands and thousands and must have been baffled. *"Philip answered, 'Two hundred denarii worth of bread wouldn't be enough for each of them to have a little'"* (John 6:7). It certainly was a mob-sized problem.

Meanwhile, Ladan had wiggled his way through the crowd to sit near the front. Perhaps he heard Jesus and Philip talking. Maybe the boy looked at his own little basket of food and thought, "What could my little amount do to help?" But, maybe he figured, after all he'd seen, Jesus could do anything! Can you picture him tugging at Andrew's sleeve to get his attention? Then with a little smile he hands Andrew his small bundle of food.

"One of His disciples, Andrew, Simon Peter's brother, said to Him, 'There's a boy here who has five barley loaves and two fish—but what are they for so many?'" (John 6:8–9).

Now logic would tell us that a small-sized meal like that would feed about five or six people, but only if they were very polite eaters. It's a good thing faith can multiply faster than logic! This is a case where everyday common reasoning limits us, but God's miracles set us free to experience the seemingly impossible.

Maybe Jesus smiled at our Laddy. *"Then Jesus said, 'Have the people sit down.' There was plenty of grass in that place, so the men sat down, numbering about five thousand. Then Jesus took the loaves, and after giving thanks He distributed them to those who were seated; so also with the fish, as much as they wanted"* (John 6:10–11).

You may want to read that again! That's right! Everybody in that crowd of thousands and thousands got more than enough to eat! Can you imagine Ladan's surprise as Jesus' disciples just kept handing out more and more fish and bread—more fish than an army of fishing boats and crews could have dragged up on shore, more bread than an entire town of bakers could have made? Fish and bread just kept coming out of the baskets, and all from Ladan's shared lunch. Now that's what I call a real kid's "Happy Meal." Ladan may have peered inside the baskets, but they all seemed ordinary enough. Boy, was his mom going to be surprised. Everybody was surprised! Everybody, that is, except Jesus. He knew all along what He was going to do.

"When they were full, He told His disciples, 'Collect the leftovers so that nothing is wasted.' So they collected them and filled twelve baskets with the pieces from the five barley loaves that were left over by those who had eaten" (John 6:12–13). Unbelievably, there were even leftovers! The crowd was amazed and, of course, extremely well fed. *"When the people saw the sign He had done, they said, 'This really is the Prophet who was to come into the world!'"* (John 6:14).

Jesus understood that the crowd was so astonished, they might do foolish things in their enthusiasm. *"Therefore, when Jesus knew that they were about to come and take Him by force to make Him king, He withdrew again to the mountain by Himself"* (John 6:15).

Ladan may have watched Jesus disappear up into the hills and marveled

JOKE

What kind of sandwich frightens easily?

A chicken sandwich.

at this day of miracles. God had taken his little offering and changed the hearts of thousands. His giving heart had helped Jesus make a difference!

There, you see, we don't need to have millions to change the world. We just have to give what we have and let God do the rest. Charity of the heart is not in how much we give, but in giving what we have. God is just as proud of you if you give a few coins as if you give millions. Generosity is the biggest treasure we have to give, and just like Ladan's few fish and loaves of bread, we never run out of it. Whether we give by donating our money, time, or talents, we can be confident that God is going to make miracles happen for people in need. If you give with a thankful, generous, and caring heart, it will always be more than enough! It doesn't take logic to add it all up. It just takes faith to make it happen!

QUESTION CORNER

* If God can feed thousands from one puny lunch, what limits do you think He has?
* What do you have that you can give?
* Can you name some charities who could use your special talents?

Energized

"Lord, may Your grace be on us, as we hope in You" (Psalm 33:22).

Many of the people Jesus healed were children who suffered from sicknesses that were slowly taking their lives away from them. Imagine that you are too sick to play or go to school and nobody knows how to help you get better; no hospitals, no doctors, no medicines can help. In fact you are so sick you may even die. Pretty scary, huh? You could say that Jesus was these children's only hope.

What exactly is hope? Hope is

putting your complete trust in someone or something. Hope is also the belief that something wonderful is going to take place even though there is no real proof that anything good can or will happen. These are the stories of two children Jesus helped in a most loving and spectacular way.

Jesus arrived in a town called Nain and discovered the people in a great state of sadness. *"Just as He neared the gate of the town, a dead man was being carried out. He was his mother's only son, and she was a widow. A large crowd from the city was also with her. When the Lord saw her, He had compassion on her and said, 'Don't cry'"* (Luke 7:12–13).

This heartbroken woman must

TRIVIA

The most common disease in Bible times was tooth decay.

have been surprised by Jesus' words; after all, she had just lost the most important person in her life. She must have been filled with such sadness and hopelessness. Her son was dead and what could change that? "Don't cry?" What was this stranger talking about?

"Then He came up and touched the open coffin, and the pallbearers stopped. And He said, 'Young man, I tell you, get up!' The dead man sat up and began to speak, and Jesus gave him to his mother. Then fear came over everyone, and they glorified God" (Luke 7:14–16). Get your money back on that coffin (hardly been used), dry those tears, and throw a party! This kid didn't need an undertaker! He was perfectly fine and quite happily undead! The crowd was stunned, and I'm surprised the guys carrying the coffin didn't drop it on the spot. His mother probably

couldn't wait to get him out of that horrid casket and into her arms! Jesus had turned a grave situation into a celebration of God's love!

Where there was complete sorrow, now there was joy and thanksgiving. The woman probably didn't know who Jesus was, and she hadn't known to trust Him, but He had touched her life and she would never forget His love.

TRIVIA

What special thing did Jesus do for Peter's mother-in-law?

He healed her of a fever.

In another town there was a man whose son was so very sick that he was close to death. This frightened father had heard about Jesus' healing powers and journeyed to Galilee to see Him. Pushing through the crowds he got close to Jesus.

"'Sir,' the official said to Him, 'come down before my boy dies!'

"'Go,' Jesus told him, 'your son will live.' The man believed what Jesus said to him and departed" (John 4:49–50).

This man had heard of Jesus and had chosen to put his hope in Him. Good choice! The man continued in his faith by believing in Jesus without proof of any miracle. He didn't need to see photo or video proof of past miracles (even if they had them), or a legal note to certify healing. He didn't even insist that Jesus come with him and prove His words. Instead, the faithful father simply trusted God.

"While he was still going down, his slaves met him saying that his boy was alive. He asked them at what time he got better. 'Yesterday at seven in the morning the fever left him,' they answered. The

father realized this was the very hour at which Jesus had told him, 'Your son will live.' Then he himself believed, along with his whole household" (John 4:51–53).

Back home, can you imagine his son's complete amazement? One minute he was burning up with fever, so terribly tired he feared he was going to die, then suddenly in the blink of an eye he was completely well. Not a trace of sickness could be seen or felt. His amazed family must have touched him over and over to see if he was truly healed. You could say it was a very touching scene!

God will do amazing things in our lives to get our attention and to build our trust and faith in Him. Suddenly, in the middle of the worst situations, God is there to comfort us, take care of us, and show us His power. It's hard to ignore God when He is doing miraculous things right in front of our eyes. Just like the widow whose son was brought back from death, we are surprised by our sudden encounters with God's powerful love. Imagine the boy explaining to the kids at school why he wasn't dead? That was an amazing show and tell. Sometimes when we're not even looking for God's help, suddenly there can be no doubting God's existence and work in our lives.

Then there is the case of the royal official. He actively sought out Jesus. The man acted only on his hope and faith that God could change the situation. He had unshakable, unquestioning trust in God.

DIDYAKNOW?

Jesus healed a blind man by putting mud on his eyes!

Do we have that same unshakeable, unquestioning trust? Or, do we need fireworks and instant changes in our lives to truly believe in God? Our faith shouldn't be based on what God can do for us. It is so easy to get in the trap of testing God. For example, if God doesn't heal your hamster, you won't believe in Him anymore. People have lost their faith due to just those types of situations. God may not heal your hamster, but that doesn't mean He doesn't love you, or worse, that He doesn't exist at all. Through good times and bad times you have to keep your faith and hope centered on God's love. God does work in our lives, and He does love us very much. God is in control of all situations, and we have to trust Him in all outcomes. And that is unquestionably and unshakably the truth!

QUESTION CORNER

* Whose faith is needed for someone to be healed?
* Does faith affect God's ability to heal? Why or why not?
* How can you be more like the faithful royal servant?

Wake-Up Fall

Start timing now! What are we timing? God. Okay, okay, we can't time God, but He does seem to be there the minute we need Him. Sometimes despite our best intentions, and even though we try our best, we still need a helping hand from God. We could call our heavenly Father our heavenly Hero! Here's a story about God really picking up the pieces when we fall short of our goals. Let's drop in on the far-off city called Troas.

A young man named Eutychus had decided to spend an evening listening to the great preacher and missionary, the apostle Paul. He must have heard many exciting stories about Paul's adventures, and now to meet him in person was like "WOW!" I think Eutychus was determined to listen to every wise word the apostle would say. He would take notes, ask questions, and sit right in the front row!

Eutychus went to a house and was directed to an upstairs room. He probably looked around in dismay. Oh no, the room was already jam-packed with people. Now he would have to sit in the back. Oh well, he could still take notes and ask questions. He found a seat

directly in front of a large open window and settled in for the meeting. *"Paul spoke to them, and since he was about to depart the next day, he extended his message until midnight"* (Acts 20:7).

At first Eutychus was concentrating on every word and probably keeping careful notes. But, I think it must have been a long day for the poor guy, for, although he found Paul a fascinating teacher, it was late and he was getting tired. He truly wanted to listen, he truly wanted to take notes, he truly wanted to ask questions, and he truly wanted to remember everything about this evening. But the crowd and the many hot lamps must have made the room very warm and stuffy. I can picture Eutychus' eyes getting heavier and sleepier. His spirit was willing but his flesh was bone tired. His head began to

droop and soon he was in a deep sleep. In his sleep Eutychus must have tilted backwards because, before you could grab a sandal, he suddenly fell straight out the third story window and down onto the ground. That's what I call really dropping off to sleep! Kerplunk! Well, you can imagine the room full of people was greatly surprised and alarmed! Especially the apostle Paul! They rushed down the stairs and out the door, but poor Eutychus was quite dead. I don't think that was the type of impact Paul wanted to make in Troas.

Well, don't just stand around gawking! We have to be ready to act the instant God needs us to, and Paul was no slowpoke. *"Paul went down, threw himself on him, embraced him, and said, 'Don't be alarmed, for his life is in him!'"* (Acts 20:10). Talk about fast action and an instant miracle! Paul, without thinking, immediately turned to prayer. Time that fast action and put it in the record books! There was no delay or asking questions. Praying was just a natural thing for Paul, because he always had his heart and mind focused on God.

An alive but confused Eutychus was helped to his feet. The last thing he could remember was listening to Paul, and then suddenly he was bungee jumping minus the cord. The happy and thankful crowd, including Eutychus, followed Paul back upstairs.

You see, we are only human, and we have weaknesses and failures.

DIDYAKNOW?

A person falling from extreme heights of over 1,880 feet can reach speeds of over 125 miles an hour.

Eutychus wanted to do his best, but he sort of dropped the ball or fell asleep on the job. But God was there to catch the problem in time and save the day. We have to learn to turn to God first—just like Paul. God was the hero of the night! Could there be any better example of God's love and power than Eutychus being raised from the dead?

There will always be times when you make mistakes or get into tough situations. They can happen in the blink of an eye, but so can God's love and help. Prayer should always be our first reaction. Prayer can be as quick as a simple SOS, but that's enough for God.

Take the true-life case of the zookeeper and a week old fawn. An injured fawn was given to a zookeeper to take care of. It was very important that the baby start drinking from a bottle right away. Try as she might, the zookeeper couldn't get the little fawn to take the bottle. The deer was getting very weak, and the zookeeper very worried. She prayed for some guidance from God. During her prayer a Bible verse (Psalm 42:1) got stuck in her head. So she looked it up. *As the deer pants for the flowing streams, so my soul pants for You, O God.* She smiled and whispered a "thank You, Lord."

Although the fawn was very young, she poured the baby formula in a large bowl and encouraged the deer to investigate. After a few uncertain tries, the baby actually started to lap the milk

DIDYAKNOW?

SOS does not mean "Save Our Souls" or "Save Our Ship." It is just the translation of a naval radio code. SOS = three dits, three dahs, and three dits.

from the bowl. God had saved the day!

We don't always succeed in our plans, even though our intentions are good, and sometimes everything we do quite literally falls apart. Prayer should always be a big part of our plans. So send up an SOS! Even if you don't always succeed on your own, God loves your willing heart and will look after you and help you do better.

QUESTION CORNER

☼ Eutychus was really eager to learn about God. How eager are you? What do you do to learn about God?

☼ Why do think God healed Eutychus?

☼ How will God treat you when you make mistakes?

Help Wanted

"I pray that your participation in the faith may become effective through knowing every good thing that is in us for Christ" (Philemon 1:4–6).

A young man named Mark was about to get his big opportunity to work with great, holy men of his time, like the missionaries Paul and Barnabas! But he was nervous and wanted to make a good impression by doing everything exactly right. But did everything turn out like he hoped? Or did Mark miss the mark? Read on!

Mark's parents' home in Jerusalem was often used as a meeting place for Christians. In fact, it was the first place

Peter went after angels sprang him from Herod's prison. With such great influences hanging around the house, young Mark soon became a strong believer in Jesus.

Barnabas and Paul were quite impressed with this young man. So, on your mark, get set, go! Pack your toothbrush and update that passport. Mark was going on a missionary adventure to far-off and exotic cities, like Antioch in Syria. He couldn't believe this outstanding invitation from his all-time heroes.

JOKE

What stays in a corner but travels all over the world? *A postage stamp.*

During their journeys, Mark's knowledge of Greek could have been very helpful, and he might have acted as their interpreter. Mark journeyed from city to city with Barnabas and Paul and had many exciting adventures. They traveled for months and hundreds of miles over land and sea. But young Mark was probably getting homesick, and it was kind of discouraging when people threw rocks at him and ran him out of town! Hey, nobody said missionary work was easy! Mark wanted to return home. Paul was extremely disappointed in his decision. Maybe he felt like Mark was just giving up. So Paul and Barnabas journeyed on, but Mark went home.

Had Mark made the wrong choice? Had he failed? That's hard to say. He definitely hadn't made a great first impression. But don't give up, Mark. Your second chance is on the way!

After returning from their journeys and spending some R&R at home, Paul and Barnabas wanted to go back on

the mission trail. Barnabas was keen on letting Mark go with them again, *"But Paul did not think it appropriate to take along this man who had deserted them in Pamphylia and had not gone with them to the work. There was such a sharp disagreement that they parted company, and Barnabas took Mark with him and sailed off to Cyprus"* (Acts 15:38–39).

Barnabas understood that Mark had been young and inexperienced before, and now a wiser Mark wanted to try again. Barnabas was willing to give him that second chance. And that second chance was all he needed. Mark turned out to be an impressive man of God, respected by everyone, including Paul.

Paul's travels led to an encounter with another pretty bright young guy! *"He went on to Derbe and Lystra, where there was a disciple named Timothy, the son of a believing Jewish woman, but his father was a Greek. The brothers at Lystra and Iconium spoke highly of him. Paul wanted him to go with him . . . As they traveled through the towns, they delivered to them the decisions reached by the apostles and elders at Jerusalem. So the churches were strengthened in the faith and were increased in number daily."* (Acts 16:1–5).

Soon Timothy became a guy Paul just couldn't do without. Paul trusted him with helping the many missions and churches in Berea, Athens, Thessalonica, and Corinth. I think Timothy just rolled up his sleeves and did his very best. When Paul was arrested and put in

DIDYAKNOW?
In Jerusalem during Jesus' time, three commonly spoken languages were Greek, Aramaic, and Hebrew.

prison in Rome, he wrote letters to busy Timothy giving advice, direction, and encouragement. Here's an example of one those letters.

"No one should despise your youth; instead you should be an example to the believers in speech, in conduct, in love, in faith, in purity. Until I come, give your attention to public reading, exhortation, and teaching. Do not neglect the gift that is in you; it was given to you through prophecy, with the laying on of hands by the council of elders. Practice these things; be involved in them, so that your progress may be evident to all. Be conscientious about yourself and your teachings; persevere in these things, for by doing this you will save both yourself and your hearers" (1 Timothy 4:12–16).

Great letter! Hey, be proud of being young and be proud about getting involved in the church just like Timothy and Mark. God doesn't expect you to know everything at once. That's why the church is full of people to help, teach, and support you just like Barnabas did for Mark.

Did you know that people are looking at you and thinking, "Hey what a great kid!" (Hey, just like I am.) I've got confidence in you because you are a talented kid! When I look out of these pages, I see a future scientist, musician, artist, preacher, or world leader, and a definite world changer. God's given you such talents and gifts! So to repeat Paul's message—don't neglect your talents! Get out into the world and show us your stuff; do

DIDYAKNOW?

One of the longest pen pal friendships on record was 75 years, from 1904 to 1979.

your very best; and follow God's plan for your life! And remember, if at first you don't succeed, try, try again. When you do, the world is going to stop, stare, and be amazed! You are going to be an awesome witness to your family, friends, teachers, coaches, and just about everybody you meet! You and God are the perfect team for success. When people see you, they are also going to see your close relationship with God and your trust in Him.

Head down to your church and see what you can to do to make a difference. Become a kid with action and attitude who works for God. People are waiting for the help only you can give and waiting to be your mentor. Don't let opportunities pass you by, because you have a mission and God has the plan. Sure it will be a challenge and an adventure, but isn't that exciting? So get out there and get into the action! Be a kid that is on the go for God! There just isn't a better way to live your life.

QUESTION CORNER

- ☀ Have you ever made the wrong choice like Mark? What helped you try again?
- ☀ Who are the people in your life that help, encourage, and mentor you? Pray for them.
- ☀ What talents has God given you for the church?

Hey, You're My Kind of Kid!

"After taking them in His arms, He laid His hands on them and blessed them" (Mark 10:16).

This story's out of order, but I thought it would be a good way to end. If you wanted to meet the president of the United States or the queen of England, you'd probably have to go through months of letters, phone calls, and arrangements. On the day of your visit, assistants would greet you and tell you to wait until that very important person had time to see you.

Jesus' disciples sometimes acted like His assistants, deciding who should see Him and when. He was constantly being followed by crowds, so the disciples were very concerned about making sure Jesus had times to eat and rest alone.

In fact, He had been having a very busy time healing the sick and preaching to the crowds. He also had to deal with suspicious Pharisees who constantly tested Him. You could say Jesus' appointment calendar was full. One day, *"Some people were bringing little children to Him so He might touch them. But His disciples rebuked them"* (Mark 10:13). Now, the disciples weren't bad fellows; they were just trying to protect Jesus. But, *"When Jesus saw it, He was indignant and said to them, 'Let the little children come to Me; don't stop them,*

DIDYAKNOW?

The story of Jesus blessing the children is also found in the books of Matthew and Luke.

for the kingdom of God belongs to such as these'" (Mark 10:14). The disciples quickly let the children step forward.

Jesus was very happy to visit with the children and spend time with them. *"'I assure you: Whoever does not welcome the kingdom of God like a little child will never enter it.' After taking them in His arms, He laid His hands on them and blessed them"* (Mark 10:15–16).

What do you suppose Jesus meant by welcoming the kingdom of God like a child? Did you know that kids have some great qualities and attitudes that adults sometimes lose as they get older? Sure!

Take the very adult Pharisees. They were constantly looking for Jesus' faults. Couldn't find any, though! But they kept testing Him, trying to trick Him. They certainly didn't receive Jesus' teachings with an open heart. They never set aside

their suspicions to really meet Jesus, and never experienced His love because they were all caught up in worldly things.

Now the children, on the other hand, came just to meet Jesus, to be held in His arms, and experience His love. They trusted Jesus with no strings attached. They had an honest kind of faith that meant just being with Jesus was enough.

Is that enough for us? Or are we constantly testing Jesus to see if He really loves us? Imagine you have a friend who constantly doubts your friendship. Every time you're together he does things to make you PROVE your friendship. It isn't enough that you want to be his friend—he always wants more. Maybe he wants you to give him your favorite toy to prove your friendship or he wants you to phone him every five minutes. His constant testing of your friendship is pretty tiring. Are we doing the same with Jesus?

Jesus is your best and most faithful friend. He always has room for you in His appointment book—day or night. There is no waiting in the hall for Jesus. He wants to spend time with you and to bless you with a good life. So trust Him completely with no doubts, worries, or tests. His friendship is forever!

QUESTION CORNER

* What is your relationship with Jesus like? Are you like a Pharisee or a child? Why?
* What are the childlike qualities that Jesus praised?
* How can your faith be more like a child's?

Conclusion

I sure had a good time exploring the adventures of kids in the Bible with you! They were brave kids who changed the world by their faith in God. In our everyday lives we may not face bullying giants, hordes of angry Philistines, or evil kings, but we do have our own challenges—big and small. It's not the kind of challenges we face that matters, but how we face them. In all situations let God be your partner and let Him in on the action. When you do, life works out better! God has a purpose and plan for you, and now's the time to start on your own personal journey with Him.

Did you know that you are important to the church too? I think I'll say that again. YOU ARE IMPORTANT! The church needs your help, your dynamic personality, and your total talent. Just like the kids in the Bible, you can make a difference. When God opens those windows of opportunity, get ready to leap into action. Hey, speaking of action, I have to talk to a new kid or two waiting to start their Bible adventures. I'll see you next time with more stories, amazing facts, and knee-slapping jokes.

L I G H T wave
building Christian faith in families

Lightwave Publishing is one of North America's leading developers of quality resources that encourage, assist, and equip parents to build Christian faith in their families. Their products help parents answer their children's questions about the Christian faith, teach them how to make church, Sunday school, and Bible reading more meaningful for their children, provide them with pointers on teaching their children to pray, and much, much more.

Lightwave, together with its various publishing and ministry partners, such as Focus on the Family, has been successfully producing innovative books, music, and games for the past 15 years. Some of their more recent products include *A Parents' Guide to the Spiritual Growth of Children*, *Joy Ride!*, *Mealtime Moments*, and *My Time With God*.

Lightwave also has a fun kids' Web site and an Internet-based newsletter called *Tips and Tools for Spiritual Parenting*. For more information and a complete list of Lightwave products, please visit: **www.lightwavepublishing.com**.